MW00910480

FRIPP WAREHOUSING
1005 Ethel Street,
Kelowna, British Coumbia,
Canada, V1Y 2W3

# Fighting the Current

Fighting the Current
Text © 2004 Heather Waldorf

Published by Lobster Press™
1620 Sherbrooke Street West, Suites C & D
Montréal, Québec   H3H 1C9
Tel. (514) 904-1100 • Fax (514) 904-1101 • www.lobsterpress.com

Publisher: Alison Fripp
Editors: Alison Fripp & Karen Li
Graphic Design & Production: Tammy Desnoyers


We acknowledge the financial support of the Government of Canada through the Book Publishing Industry Development Program (BPIDP) for our publishing activities.

The Canada Council | Le Conseil des Arts
for the Arts | du Canada

We acknowledge the support of the Canada Council for the Arts for our publishing program.


National Library of Canada Cataloguing in Publication


Waldorf, Heather, 1966-

  Fighting the current / Heather Waldorf.


ISBN 1-894222-93-8 (bound).--ISBN 1-894222-92-X (pbk.)


  I. Title.

PS8645.A458F53 2004          C813'.6          C2004-901698-9

Printed and bound in Canada.

*For Talia, who loves words and wildlife.*

– Heather Waldorf

# Fighting the Current

written by
HEATHER WALDORF

Lobster Press™

# Part 1

To stick your hands into the river is to feel the cords that bind
the earth together in one piece.

– Barry Lopez

# Chapter 1

I'm not sure what it was that first intrigued me about the new kid, Ethan Stinson, but I could think of plenty of "its" that might have repelled me had I not been a good sport.

For starters, he was a genius, scoring an unheard of ninety-nine per cent on Mr. "Killer" Fitzpatrick's annual back-to-school, *"Welcome to Advanced Algebra—Let's See How Long You Last"* pop quiz. I was merely clever, coming in second at a distant, *measly*, ninety-four. What I had always assumed was a reserved seat at the top of North Creek High's list of Ontario Scholars was pulled out from under me by a tall, bespectacled farm kid fresh from Newfoundland. Standing behind Ethan in line to receive our battle-scarred algebra textbooks, I could almost feel my brain shrinking.

And Ethan wasn't just smart; he was funny, too. That same first day, Ms. Withers launched a discussion about one of the novels on the required summer reading list for English—a list Ethan couldn't possibly have received having just registered at North Creek that morning. I raised my hand and asked a question about one of the novel's minor characters, Mr. Toaste.

Ms. Withers turned the question back to the class. "Can

anyone answer Theresa's question about Mr. Toaste?"

"Where does he pop up in the novel?" asked a deep, unfamiliar voice from the back row.

I whipped my head around. Ethan winked at me, and despite the fact his quip was cornier than a can of niblets, I laughed out loud. Everyone stared. It had been so long since anyone had tried to make me laugh. But Ethan didn't know my life was a mess, or that his comment had prompted my first real smile in a long time. In months. All summer, in fact. It was only the afternoon of the first day of school and I was already sick of people tiptoeing around me, talking in whispers, patting me on the shoulder, and telling me not to worry, that everything would be just fine. As if.

It was probably that innocent effort at humour, not Ethan's high cheekbones, his long, sun-streaked hair, or the rugged way he filled out his patched Levi's and faded hand-knit sweater that caused the odd *ping, ping, ping* sensation in my chest that afternoon when I realized he and I had lockers side by side.

"Hey, Theresa Stanford," he said, later that week. It was three o'clock, Friday afternoon and Ethan was extracting a green polar fleece jacket from his locker. I was unenthusiastically loading my knapsack with a weekend's worth of homework assignments.

"You can call me Tee," I said.

Ethan raised a brow. "Tee? Just letter T? Or Tea, like iced tea?"

"Like golf tee," I replied.

"You play golf?" Ethan asked.

I shook my head. "I worked the refreshment booth one

summer at Morrie's Mini-Putt out on the highway. Morrie had 'Tee' embroidered on my staff shirt as a gag. It caught on." Truth was only my teachers, my mother, and my Aunt George still called me Theresa. My father Mel used to call me by my full name, Theresa-Jean, but now he called me Tee, too. Tee, the Weekend Visitor.

"So, Miss Golf Tee, you have a ride home?" Ethan asked, zipping up his jacket.

"Of course," I replied, reaching for my red bike helmet on the top shelf of my locker. My ten-speed was outside on the rack. That was the week JC School Transportation Services went on strike, leaving everyone but the townies to make alternative arrangements. Just my luck. Since school started, I'd been driving Mel's old Jeep to and from classes, but I'd dropped it off at the auto shop the previous afternoon to get a noisy muffler replaced. It wouldn't be ready for pickup until Monday.

"It's pouring rain. You live far?" Ethan asked.

"Birch Lane. It's off River Road." It was eight kilometres from town, mostly uphill.

"You'll get drenched," Ethan grinned.

I shrugged. I didn't want to be rude, but I'd had a tough week and was in no mood to play nice with the new guy.

Ethan ignored my efforts to repel him. "I was about to head home; there's a crap-load of unpacking to do and the kitchen sink needs repairs. Why don't you let me drop you off? You can toss your bike in the bed of my pickup."

There was something endearing about the way, despite his superior grey matter, Ethan tossed around redneck terms like "crap-load." And he hardly seemed the serial killer sort. "Well, okay. Sure. If it's not out of your way," I said, realizing I had no idea where he lived; North Creek drew students from a fifteen-mile radius.

Ethan shook his head. "I'm just a little further along River Road, out past Cedar Bend, near the locks. You know it? Old, white farmhouse, kind of rundown?"

I nodded. "It's the old Harper place. Mr. Harper's wife died a year ago and he went to stay with his grown children in the city."

Ethan smirked. "Small towns are the same everywhere. Everybody knows everything about everyone."

"It's a mixed blessing."

"Hey," Ethan asked. "You don't live near that enormous log house on Birch Lane, do you? The one with the big stained glass windows and the huge carved animals on the porch? I passed it a few times over the weekend. It's really something."

"I don't live *near* it; it's home-sweet-home—at least for now," I said, then sheepishly explained, "I'm really a townie. I grew up a ten-minute walk from here, in a bungalow near the college. My Aunt George owns the house out on Birch Lane."

"Aunt *George*? Let me guess, it's *Uncle* George, but he likes to wear leather miniskirts and fishnets around the house," Ethan hooted.

"Sorry to disappoint you," I grinned despite myself. "It's Aunt *Georgina*. I've been staying with her while my dad's away."

Sure, Tee, I thought, make it sound like Mel was on a big shot business trip or vacationing in the sunny south. Make him sound like a man who went exciting places. Truth was, my father was a guy who went ordinary places. At the worst possible times.

Like that Saturday morning when I was eleven and he took our old beagle Jake for a walk through Riverside Park. He rounded the bend near the Witch's Tree at exactly the same moment Leona Brown and I were crouched behind the old oak swapping drags of a Players Light Leona had stolen from her mother's purse. I was grounded for a month, a punishment made worse by the fact Mel wasn't usually strict; in fact, I was accustomed to having him wrapped tightly around my baby finger. I didn't tell Mel I'd been repulsed by the hot, bitter taste of the cigarette and wasn't likely to try it again. I let him assume his lengthy health sermons and weeks of house arrest had done the trick, made me a better person, and directed me towards a smoke-free adolescence. I figured his over-the-top reaction to my tobacco trial was because he cared about me. Whether he still did was anybody's guess.

Another time, when I was fourteen, Mel came home early from his job teaching biology at the local college with a sore throat and a half-day's worth of papers to mark. He found my mother Lucy, an aerobics instructor at the River's Edge Athletic Club, in the kitchen practicing what appeared to be a naked, high-impact routine with her then-boss Harold. After the divorce, my mother broke it off with Harold, left town, moved into a small Toronto condo, and got work teaching fitness classes at the North York YMCA.

There was never any question of me going to live with my mother; we'd never been close. Petite, graceful, and artistic, Lucy couldn't relate to her rambunctious tomboy daughter who chose hockey and volleyball over gymnastics and figure skating lessons. Who despised the art workshops, music classes, and old movies she was so eager for me to enjoy. Whose favourite childhood pastime had been bogging for bullfrogs with Dad in the creek behind our house. From the beginning of tenth grade until that gut-wrenching summer before my senior year, I made a four-hour, obligatory bus trip to Toronto the third weekend of each month.

My mother and I would spend our time together at theatres, malls, and noisy restaurants, places where heartfelt conversation could be avoided. We told each other only good things. Lucy would talk about her job, new clothes she'd bought, interesting novels she'd read. I told her about my exam scores, my class trip to Montreal, how I'd aced my driver's license test. If my mother had male friends, *any* friends, she never mentioned them. I never mentioned how Joey Montague, my first real boyfriend, dumped me for an Ottawa girl. Or how disappointed Mel was, and I was, when I messed up at tryouts and had to give up a coveted spot on the North Creek Senior Girl's hockey team.

I never told Lucy that, despite our differences, I missed her sometimes. Or how I worried Mel would never find another woman to love. That no sane female would take on a balding single father who wore formaldehyde the way other men wore Old Spice. Who, after the divorce, spent every Saturday night in the garage puttering away at what he called his "life's major to-do project"—designing and building a cedar strip canoe. He'd promised that the spring of my senior year, we'd paddle it from Kingston to Ottawa, the entire length of the Rideau Waterway, camping and visiting the historic lock stations and small towns along the way.

But then, ten weeks ago, at seven a.m., the Friday before the start of the Canada Day weekend, Mel was again at the right place, at the wrong time. On his way to teach summer school, my father was leaving the Country Corner Coffee Shop with his usual pre-class coffee and cinnamon-raisin bagel when Jerry Smythe, the local hell-raiser, rounded the aforementioned country corner, jumped the curb, and ran Mel over. Jerry, who'd been driving home from a night of partying in the city, who'd been driving with a suspended license following a string of prior DWI's, was thrown in jail to await trial. Mel, after emerging from a three-week coma, was sent to do indefinite time at the Eastern Ontario Rehabilitation Centre in nearby Ottawa. His cuts and fractures healed well enough, but a closed head injury left Mel with the language and problem-solving   abilities of a five-year-old and the tasks of having to relearn how to walk, feed himself, and use the toilet independently. Aunt George and the doctors were optimistic Mel would gain back most of his skills, but I would've been happy if my father could even remember I was his kid, not just the girl he'd learned to call "Tee" because he couldn't pronounce "Theresa-Jean" anymore.

"Let's roll," Ethan said, interrupting my dark thoughts. He grabbed my knapsack from the floor, grunted, and passed it over to me. "What do you have in there? Bricks? Dumbbells? Gold bars?"

"Homework, gym shoes, library books..."

"You'll give yourself a hunchback biking around like that."

"That would be the least of my problems," I mumbled.

Ethan's ancient pickup was probably dark blue, but who could tell under the layers of muck. The cabin smelled of wet blankets and the vinyl bench seat was cracked and duct-taped in several places. Ethan spent a good two minutes resuscitating the engine, and another fiddling with the off-beat windshield wipers.

"My pride and joy," he grinned, patting the dusty dash-board. "Old Wilma brought me all the way from The Rock. She complained, *loudly*, the entire way, but I love her all the same."

"How do you like living here?" I asked as we chugged out of North Creek's student parking lot and made our way through town towards the highway.

Ethan shrugged. "It's a nice piece of land we have, much bigger than back in Stephenville, though not really big enough to make a go at full-time farming. Dad's itching to fish on the river. My sister Ellie took riding lessons at summer day camp and has been campaigning for a horse. Mom likes the big kitchen and the lot full of sugar maples."

"But how do *you* like living here?" I asked again.

Ambivalence etched Ethan's brow. "It absolutely sucks having to start over in a new place my last year of high school. But at the same time I'm closer now to a bunch of good universities. I've got my eye on Queen's." He laughed. "Of course, old Wilma here might need an engine transplant before she'll commit herself to a regular two-hour commute. I may end up at U of O."

"Why did your family choose North Creek?" I asked. "It's such a small town and so far from Newfoundland. You have relatives here?"

Ethan shook his head. "My sister has CF."

"CF?"

"Cystic Fibrosis. It's genetic. It affects Ellie's lungs and digestive system. As she gets older, she'll get sicker, maybe need a gastrostomy or lung transplant. My parents have been saving for years to move her closer to a major children's hospital with a CF clinic; CHEO, in Ottawa, is only forty-five minutes from North Creek. Dad found the farm and a job in town with help from a CF parents' group he joined on-line. He starts today as the new supervisor of outdoor maintenance at the college. Grass cutting. Snow removal. Building repairs. He likes outdoor work, even though he knows it'll never make him rich. I'm counting on scholarships and some good part-time jobs to get me through university."

"What field do you want to study?"

"Genetics," Ethan replied with fire in his eyes. "I'm going to find a cure for Ellie's disease."

"How old is she?" I asked.

"Twelve. She's in seventh grade. Misses too much school to take it seriously, but she's the most creative kid I know; she paints, sings, plays piano by ear, copies dance moves she sees on MuchMusic."

"How does she manage all that with her illness?" I didn't want to pry, but I was interested and Ethan seemed open to talk, enthusiastic even. I'd never had a sibling. I knew kids who despised theirs, but Ethan had an open affection for Ellie that made me wonder, not for the first time, if I was missing something being an only child.

"Ellie takes more than fifty pills a day: oral antibiotics to ward off lung infections, enzymes to help digest her food, vitamins to boost her immunity. She needs bronchodilators three times daily through an aerosol mask. And there's what's called 'postural drainage,' a series of chest percussions done morning and night to loosen thick mucous buildup in her lungs. It's time consuming, but it keeps Ellie pretty healthy and active."

"And CF can't be cured?" I asked, awed that Ethan described the medications and procedures in such a matter-of-fact way. *Fifty pills a day?* I had trouble swallowing the occasional Tylenol.

Ethan shook his head. "Not yet, but Ellie has a good shot at making it to adulthood, maybe into her forties. Her disease will never get better, but the treatments can slow it down. Sorry, I talk too much. We're getting close to Birch Lane, right?"

"Next right," I pointed.

"It's a beautiful home," Ethan said as the log house came into view.

"Thanks," I replied. "My aunt designed it herself. I can show you the inside if you'd like."

Ethan hesitated, chewing his lip.

I laughed. "It's okay; Aunt George isn't home. If she were, she'd probably offer you a few grand to take me on a date. She doesn't think it's normal for a seventeen-year-old girl not to have a boyfriend. But trust me, I have enough troubles without one."

"Good," Ethan grinned. "Because I already have a girlfriend."

That took me aback. "You work fast."

He laughed, then shook his head. "My girlfriend's back East, in Newfoundland."

"Must be hard, being so far away," I mused.

"She's right here," Ethan said, pointing to his shirtfront.

"She's in your pocket?"

"She's in my heart."

"How romantic," I grinned.

"Shut up," Ethan laughed.

Aunt George's house was nothing short of spectacular if you didn't mind living on a winding dirt road eight kilometres from the nearest grocery store. She didn't; in fact, that's why she lived there. With her bucks, Aunt George could have lived anywhere in the world, but she loved the quiet, the trees, and the Rideau River a literal stone's throw from her back porch.

When I was a toddler, my father's much-older sister was a good-humoured widow working for peanuts as a receptionist at an Ottawa dental office. She started writing murder mysteries at night to pass the time and ward off what she called "menopausal angst." She never expected to make any money at it, never entertained possibilities of becoming a literary diva. But she became *the* Georgina Simmons, best-selling mystery writer, author of the "Midnight Jones" series, among others. Her novels were stocked in every bookshop, grocery store, and 7-Eleven in North America and had been translated into seventeen languages worldwide: one had even been made into a TV movie starring Pamela Anderson.

Several years back, when strangers started recognizing Aunt George from book jacket photos and stalking her for autographs on the streets of Ottawa, she decided it might soon be time to return to the back roads of nearby North Creek, the town where she and Mel grew up. She wasn't comfortable in the urban spotlight, preferring the company of family and friends who knew her before she became a writer and who still treated her like the funny, slightly eccentric outdoorswoman she used to be and would be again. Instead of house hunting immediately, Aunt George started taking university courses on-line. Her real dream, she admitted, was to be an architect.

Aunt George's house on Birch Lane was the full-scale realization of her dream home as she'd envisioned it as a young girl, inspired no doubt by her grandparents' old summer cottage in Haliburton where she and Mel spent a month each summer as children. "Big dreams, a strong back, good drafting skills, and oodles of cash are a mighty combination," she told Mel when she called to say she'd bought an old vacant property beside the river. Six months later, she gave up her Ottawa condo for good when she, my father, and a slew of top-of-the-line contractors finished creating what she simply called "The Cabin."

*"Cabin?"* Ethan exclaimed as he parked the truck in the

turnaround and followed me up the slate walkway.

From the outside, Aunt George's home was a sprawling two-story log mansion with a wraparound porch furnished with hand-painted Muskoka chairs and her ever-growing collection of life-size wooden animal carvings. The moose, wolf, black bear, cougar, and grizzly were beautiful in the daylight, but at night they seemed a little disconcerting, which may have been the point. Aunt George hated the idea of spoiling her property's rustic charm with gates, security cameras, and alarms. She assumed any aggressive trespassers not put off by her snarling wooden menagerie would be "loved" into submission by Harley, her boisterous Great Dane.

Inside, the house was no less impressive. The ground floor was high ceilinged and open-concept, with the kitchen, dining, and living areas all blending seamlessly into one another. In keeping with her Outdoor Canadiana theme, Aunt George's floors were hardwood, her fireplaces stone. Prints by Bateman, Carr, and the Pratts graced the walls. Two octagonal stained glass windows, designed by a local artist, depicted Mallards in flight and cast colourful images on the kitchen floor in the early morning light. The upstairs was divided into several rooms: a large den full of books and easy chairs; three bedrooms, each with private baths and small outdoor balconies overlooking the river; and a multipurpose studio where Aunt George wrote her mysteries and did her architectural assignments. A basement gym sported cardio machines, free weights, and a lap pool.

"If the circumstances under which I came to stay had been different, I'd think I was in heaven," I laughed.

Ethan raised a brow. "You said your dad was *away*?"

I was rescued from further explanation by a stampede of heavy footsteps bounding down the stairs towards our voices.

"It's Aunt George's puppy," I explained, realizing Harley must have been outside when Ethan and I came in. Aunt George always left an upstairs balcony door open so Harley could get fresh air when no one was home. "Brace yourself. Harley doesn't know her own strength."

Nine-month-old Harley galloped into the basement and threw all hundred pounds of her lanky black and white body at Ethan in the obnoxiously affectionate greeting she reserved for all visitors; just last week, she'd knocked an elderly Avon lady to the ground. Aunt George and I were trying to teach the high-spirited Harley some basic commands, some self-control, but she was a hard sell, a shameless flirt.

I yelled a futile "Harley, down!" but Ethan just laughed, ruffled her ears, and scratched her belly. His friendly efforts were rewarded with a sloppy tongue bath.

"First time I've been French kissed by a Great Dane," Ethan said, wiping his face on his sleeve.

I didn't want to think about Ethan and French kissing simultaneously. I had enough to make me crazy without losing it over some guy. Especially some guy with a girlfriend. Ethan and I could be friends. Good friends. *Just* friends.

Harley gave Ethan a final nuzzle, then with a flick of her tail she bounded back up the stairs to the kitchen. I heard her slurping water out of her giant stainless steel bowl, then the familiar *ker-plunk* as she stretched out on the cool ceramic tiles for an afternoon nap. I envied Harley's life.

I laughed. "I can imagine what Harley might do to some poor, unsuspecting guy once she's full grown."

"That's a strange name for a she-pup," Ethan said.

"Aunt George got her last spring from a guy who ran a classified: 'Great Dane puppy needs more time, space, patience, and dog food than I can afford. Free to a good home.' The guy delivered her in a wire crate rigged to the back of his motorcycle. Also, her splotchy black and white colouring is called 'Harlequin.'"

"Is she a purebred?"

I nodded, "Pure pain in the butt." But I didn't mean it. If only Ethan knew how many times over the summer I'd cried into Harley's fur, walking her for hours along the river, searching for answers to questions I was afraid to ask Aunt George about Mel's chances for a full recovery. For as long as I remembered, Aunt George had been *the* one to go to if I wanted honest answers about anything from drugs to world politics. Her honesty was sometimes gentle, sometimes brutal; either way, I'd grown up accepting it as the truth. But when it came to Mel, I couldn't handle any more "truths." Harley kept me sane, answering all my questions with reassuring licks to my hand and enthusiastic wags of her tail. I loved that pain in the butt.

"Thanks for the ride," I said when Ethan and I made it back to the front door.

"Thanks for showing me the house. I feel like I was teleported into an episode of 'Lifestyles of the Rich and Famous,'" he grinned.

"Aunt George plays down the celebrity thing," I explained. "She grew up in North Creek. In town, she's just the same old Georgina she was before, and I quote, 'the writing bug bit her on the ass and wouldn't let go.'"

Ethan laughed. "Tee," he asked, "do you have a lab partner for Chemistry yet?"

I shook my head. Mr. Harnett said we could choose our own partners and submit names the following week. In the past, when given a choice of partners for class projects, I'd paired up with my friend Leona Brown, but she moved with her family to Saskatoon last spring.

"Want to work together?" Ethan asked. "You seem to know your stuff."

There was no point in letting him know I had to study my butt off to learn what seemed to come naturally to him. I had yet to see Ethan crack a book in class; he was too busy cracking jokes.

"Sure," I replied, my chest doing that odd *ping, ping, ping* thing again. Get a grip, I told myself. Just because he wants to be your lab partner doesn't mean the two of you have, well, *chemistry*.

"See you in school, then." Ethan waved and headed down the porch stairs. "Bye, Kitty," he added, scratching behind the wooden ears of the life-size cougar perched on the railing.

I followed him to the turnaround and waved him off. Walking back towards the empty house, I caught a glimpse of the big shed down by the river.

I hadn't taken Ethan out back on purpose. If he'd asked what was in the shed, I would have told him it was no big deal, that it held tools, the riding lawnmower, the snow blower, and an old rowboat. But truth was, it also housed the hull of the sixteen-foot cedar strip canoe that Mel, with my help, had almost finished at the time of what people liked to call "the accident." We'd had plans to install seats, add the trim, and apply coats of varnish over the summer, then test-paddle it along the creek that meandered behind our bungalow and through town. But now our house was rented out and the canoe was in storage here at Aunt George's along with some furniture and other tangible vestiges of my previous life. It, like my father, like myself, now had an uncertain future.

# Chapter 2

A few moments later, Aunt George roared into the double garage.

She bustled into the house, her arms full of groceries. "Was that a *boy* pulling out of the driveway?" Her blue eyes twinkled. The thought of me sneaking guys into the house when she was out delighted her; she worried I'd become too much of a loner.

"That was Ethan, a new guy at school. His family just moved into the old Harper farm past Cedar Bend. It was raining so he gave me a ride home."

Aunt George grinned. "Hmm. A new guy. I wish I'd had a chance to meet him."

"He's too young for you," I said.

Aunt George, tall, big-boned, and strong as an ox from a lifetime of outdoor hobbies, whacked me playfully on the shoulder. "You know that's not what I meant. Is he cute? I couldn't get a good look past all the mud on his windshield."

"He's nice-looking; he's nice, *period*. Don't give me that look; Ethan has a girlfriend."

"If he just moved here, it couldn't be anything serious."

I sighed. "She's back in Newfoundland. That's where he's from."

Aunt George was nonplussed. "Maybe it won't last," she said, pulling open the refrigerator door. "Long-distance love is sometimes too much work."

She should know. My Uncle Stan had been a travelling salesman, on the road six days a week, fifty weeks a year. He died of a heart attack a month before their divorce was finalized.

"Enough about Ethan," I said. "How was Dad today?" Aunt George visited Mel Tuesday and Friday mornings; I went all day on Saturdays. Like me, she'd gone to see Mel every day all summer. But I was back in school now, Aunt George was behind with her writing and architecture assignments, and Mel was busy with physiotherapy, occupational therapy, speech therapy, and recreation therapy. The effort tired him out and made him irritable sometimes. One of the family counsellors at the Centre suggested it would be best for all of us if Aunt George and I cut down on the visits a little, try to get back into our old routines, and let Mel get enough rest. His progress was slow but it had been steady, and we were all hoping he'd be able to come home to Aunt George's for a visit by Christmas.

"Good," Aunt George replied, her ample backside to me as she tossed veggies and fruits into the crisper. "The physiotherapist got Mel to take a little stroll with the walker today."

"How did he do?"

"He made it from the bed to the bathroom. It took half an hour of step, rest, step, rest, but it's an improvement from last week. Mel's reading is getting better, too; still picture books, but his comprehension is good if you ask questions about the story afterwards. The speech therapist said it's great you've been reading more advanced stories to him."

"We're starting the second Harry Potter book tomorrow,"

I replied. "Or I might try him with *The Apprenticeship of Duddy Kravitz.* I need to read it this weekend for English."

Aunt George shut the refrigerator door and tucked a strand of curly, silver hair behind her ear. "Mel said something strange today, Theresa."

This was hardly earth-shattering news. Mel's Ph.D. in biology was useless now, but he'd become a master at gibberish.

Aunt George explained, "I wheeled him into the lounge to watch 'Live with Regis and Kelly.' When today's date was mentioned, Mel looked over at me, grinned like a kid, and started humming the 'Happy Birthday' song. It's not *my* birthday, or yours, or his, so I asked him, 'Whose birthday is it, Mel?' He gave me this look, like I should know better. 'I love Lucy' he said. 'You want to watch "I Love Lucy"?' I asked, wondering if the hospital even got the Retro Channel. Then he just shook his head and retreated into himself the way he does now when he gets confused or frustrated."

I stopped listening to Aunt George when she got to the part about Mel saying "I Love Lucy."

I took a deep breath. "Aunt George, it's Mom's birthday today. *Lucy's.*"

Aunt George frowned. "Really?"

I nodded excitedly. "I totally forgot about Mom's birthday. Dad hasn't called her 'I Love Lucy' since I was a little kid…. *He remembered Lucy!*" I shouted, jumping up and down.

Aunt George's face lit up like a Christmas tree. She joined me in a little dance around the kitchen. "He's coming back, Tee! The doctor's have always said Mel's memories would probably return gradually, in snippets, that they might come and go, that his first memories might not be the obvious ones."

"I better call Mom after dinner," I said, suddenly sober.

Aunt George calmed, too, and put her hands on my shoulders. "You should go and *see* her soon, Theresa. It's been too long."

"I don't know," I said.

"It's your decision."

I sighed. "A tough one."

Aunt George shook her head and pulled me into a hug. "Not really. Just do what's in your heart."

The last time I'd seen or spoken to my mother was three days after Mel was hospitalized. She'd driven straight from Toronto the minute Aunt George had called her to let her know what had happened. For three days Lucy stayed with us at the hospital while the doctors resuscitated and operated on Mel, set his bones, stabilized him, and informed us he was in a deep coma. There was little to be done, they said, until if and when he regained consciousness and more tests could be run to determine the extent of the brain injury.

"We'd better go back to the house and get you packed," Lucy had said.

"Aunt George can take me by to pick up some stuff tomorrow," I'd replied, assuming I'd be staying with her the way I usually did when Mel needed to be away overnight. I was exhausted, and now that Mel was out of immediate danger I just wanted to get some sleep. Stupidly, it never crossed my mind that Lucy assumed I'd travel back to Toronto with her.

"She's welcome to stay with me, Lucy," Aunt George had said.

But Lucy turned on me. "I'm still your mother, Theresa, and you're barely seventeen. The custody agreement states, quite clearly, that if something were to happen to Mel I would automatically assume full-time parental responsibilities."

"I can't leave Dad now. He needs me. You can't just change my life without his input!" I insisted.

Lucy put her arm around me and said gently but without much tact, "What if he dies, Theresa? Or is paralyzed? Your life has changed whether you like it or not. We'll come back each weekend for as long as he's in the hospital, sooner if we have to," —I knew she meant if he died— "Now, please, say goodbye to Georgina and let's go. It's a long drive."

I'd held myself together pretty well thus far, given the horrific circumstances. But Lucy's bluntness burst the pent-up dam of anxiety within me; dark, overwhelming emotions surged like a flash flood.

To put it mildly, I *freaked*, right there in the ICU waiting room. I cried, yelled, ranted, threw magazines, and pushed my mother and Aunt George away when they tried to calm me. I scared the hell out of everyone in the room, myself included.

Security was summoned and I was dragged kicking and screaming into an examining room by two burly orderlies. A doctor rushed in and gave me a shot in the hip that knocked me senseless.

When I woke up a few hours later, a prissy-looking social worker was talking with my mother at my bedside. Miss Priss informed me that given the unusual circumstances, it had been agreed that I would stay with Aunt George, for now. That it would be best for me to be near my father during his recovery (she didn't say *if* he recovered). That I should keep my summer job, the one my father pulled strings to get me, as a counsellor at a day camp sponsored by the Ottawa Museum of Science and Technology. That it might be difficult and not in my best interest to start my senior year at a huge and unfamiliar Toronto high school.

Though resigned, Lucy was still upset, her face red and bloated from crying. "I better go now, Theresa," she'd sniffed. "I know your aunt will take good care of you. Please let me know if you need anything." *Sniff.* "Please call if you want to talk." *Sniff.* "We haven't always understood each other, and I've made a lot of mistakes, but I love you, Theresa." *Double sniff.* "I know you are angry now, and I'm so sorry I upset you, but please remember my door's always open." *Sniff, sniff, sniff.*

The social worker passed Lucy a tissue.

"Bye, Mom," I'd mumbled, barely able to look at her.

It had been more than two months since that day, but I still felt nauseous about my meltdown at the hospital, ashamed I hadn't found the courage to apologize for my blow-up. I felt terrible that, after my mother left, Miss Priss asked me why I'd been so hysterical at the thought of living with my mother. *Was it because she abused you?* Offended for my mother's sake, I yelled, "Don't you understand that I need to stay with my father? Has *your* father ever been in a coma? Well, *has he*?" I waited, and finally the social worker shook her head. I continued, "If my mother still lived in North Creek, I'd be happy to stay with her." "Happy" was perhaps an over-statement, but Miss Priss didn't need to know that.

The social worker nodded, pretending to understand my frustration. She folded up my file, looked at her watch, and stood up. "Whenever you're ready, Theresa, your aunt is waiting to take you home."

I waited until after dinner to call Lucy. Since it was Friday night, not to mention her birthday, I wasn't sure she'd even be home. Maybe she'd be out with friends. Maybe she had a date. Maybe I'd luck out and get her answering machine.

"Hi, Mom," I said when she picked up after three rings.

"Theresa?" There was surprise in her voice. "Is that you?"

I'd done the math. "Happy thirty-seventh!"

"Ssh! Don't remind me," Lucy laughed.

I don't know what she had to feel old about. Lucy was three months shy of twenty, a second-year kinesiology major at McGill, when I was born. Mel was a grad student and had been Lucy's first-year Anatomy T.A. It didn't take a rocket scientist to figure out how their tutorial time was spent or which parts of their anatomy were studied up close and personal.

"How are you, Theresa?" Lucy asked. "How's school?" She sounded as eager as I to put that wretched day last summer behind us.

"I'm okay. School's okay. Dad's doing better," I added cautiously.

Lucy said, "I know, Theresa. I've been to see him a few times."

I was floored. "You have?"

"Just because you divorce someone doesn't mean you stop caring about them."

"I've never seen you there," I said defensively. What I really wanted to know was why she hadn't come to see me, too. But part of me already knew the answer.

She was honest. "I went later in the evenings, after you and Georgina left. I didn't know if my being there would upset you again."

"Does Aunt George know you've been to visit Mel?"

"Of course. She calls me every week to let me know how he's doing and how you're doing, too." Lucy paused.

"I've wanted to talk to you, Theresa, to try and make things better between us, but I didn't want to risk setting you off again when you were already so anxious about Mel. I hoped you'd call when you were ready."

Anger swelled in my chest. I hated that my mother thought I was this fragile, explosive kid now, and that Aunt George hadn't confided she'd been in touch with Lucy. But just as quickly, my anger deflated. I knew having another temper tantrum wasn't going to accomplish anything.

"Can I come down to see you next weekend?" I asked, instead. "I'd like to bring your birthday present." I hadn't bought one yet, but she didn't need to know that.

"Visiting will be gift enough, Theresa," Lucy said, her voice lifting. "Should I meet the bus or train next Friday?"

I thought about it a second. "Friday's a P.D. day," I remembered. "I don't have school, so I'll arrange to visit Mel in the morning with Aunt George and then drive down to Toronto in time for dinner. I'll take you to Red Lobster for a belated birthday dinner."

"You'll *drive*?" Lucy asked.

"Mel's pretty generous these days about lending me the Jeep."

Lucy was quiet a moment, no doubt debating whether to warn me against Toronto's nasty rush hour traffic. Finally she said, "I'll reserve you a parking pass. Drive carefully, Theresa. I'm looking forward to seeing you."

I took a deep breath. "I've missed you, Mom," I said quickly, then hung up before she could respond.

# Chapter 3

The next afternoon I was sitting cross-legged at the end of Mel's bed finishing some algebra homework while he watched "The Simpsons" and fed himself a bowl of chocolate pudding with a built-up spoon. He'd spilled some on his chin, but the occupational therapist told me not to wipe it for him. My job was to hold up the mirror when he finished and encourage him to wipe it himself.

I was stumped by the last algebra problem. Three months ago, Mel would have helped me, seen the answer right away, and talked me through it. Today, when his cartoons were over, I held the problem up in front of his face just for fun; remarkably, his eyesight was still 20/20. Mel looked at the problem for a good three minutes, then said, "Uh...mmm...gee....four?" He snickered like he didn't have a care in the world. "Read me some more of the wizard book?"

"What do you want for dinner, Dad?" I asked, my voice hoarse after an hour of reading aloud. The Centre staff let me rent videos and order in for him on Saturday nights.

Mel used to like dramas and documentaries; now he liked cartoons and Jim Carrey movies. I'd sat through *The Cable Guy* and *How the Grinch Stole Christmas* so many times that summer I was ready to pull my hair out.

"Macaroni," Mel said.

"Macaroni?" I asked. "And cheese? You want *Kraft Dinner*?" Yuck, I thought.

Mel frowned and gave me a look like it was me with the head injury.

"Macaroni Pizza."

I sighed with relief. "*Pepperoni* Pizza?"

Mel nodded and grinned. He liked kiddie food now. Hot dogs. McNuggets. Fish sticks. Pizza. I'd know he was feeling like his old self again when he asked for a sirloin steak (medium rare), baked potato (sour cream on the side) and a spinach salad (hold the dressing).

Later that evening, while Mel giggled his way through *Ace Ventura: Pet Detective*, I worked out the elusive algebra problem. Shocked, I flipped to the answer code at the back of the textbook to double-check. *Four*. The answer was *four*. I sat back, amazed. Was my father finally coming around? I watched him as he stared wide-eyed with delight at Jim Carrey and oblivious to the string of drool hanging from his chin. Fat chance, I concluded. But what if...? Nah.

When visiting hours were over, I helped Mel to the bathroom, and then tucked him into bed. I gathered my belongings together, kissed his cheek, and told him I'd come the following Friday instead of Saturday, not that the days of the week meant much to him anymore.

"I'm going to see Mom next weekend," I said, waiting to see if I'd get a reaction.

"Mom?" It wasn't the answer I wanted. He didn't remember.

I tried not to show my frustration, but sometimes I couldn't help myself. "Mom. Lucy. Your *ex-wife*. Remember, her birthday was yesterday?" I started humming "Happy Birthday," hoping it would jar his memory.

Mel's face was blank.

I let it go and kissed him again. "I love you, Dad. See you in a few days."

"Tee?" he said when I was almost at the door.

I wanted him to say he loved me back, say he was still proud to be my dad, say something, *anything*, that would let me know I was more to him than Tee, the Weekend Visitor.

I turned back.

"Four," he said and held up one, two, three, four fingers.

"You're right, Dad. The answer was four. Good work. Get some sleep."

During the forty-five minute ride back to Aunt George's, I listened to Ottawa's country music station. I wasn't a fan of country music, but it was what Mel listened to when he drove, and I didn't have the heart to change his radio to the pop rock station I preferred. Or the guts to admit his driving days were over.

Manoeuvring through Ottawa's west end to the 416, I watched other young people on the streets, in cars, waiting for the OC Transpo. They were going on dates, coming home from a day of shopping at Carlingwood, meeting friends at Laps Sports Bar to watch the first game of the World Series. I'd just spent twelve hours in a rehab hospital with a man I loved dearly who didn't know who I was. I was going home to run a few kilometres on the treadmill to sweat out the day's stress, take a long hot shower, and try to sleep. Some nights I lay awake for hours worried that my father could still die, worried that this child-man he'd become was here to stay. I knew I should be grateful that Mel was alive, accept him for who he was now, but it was so hard, *too* hard. I wanted my dad back. I wanted to help him finish the canoe. I wanted to move back to our little bungalow in town. I wanted to discuss frog guts over dinner again. I wanted my normal life back, dammit.

Then I worried I was being selfish, that I should stop feeling sorry for myself, stop resenting all the unexpected and unwelcome changes in my life. After all, I wasn't the only kid who spent Saturdays at the Centre. Some of the other kids' parents were even worse off than Mel.

It was only recently that I'd begun to hope. Hope that Mel might make a full recovery. Hope that if he didn't, we'd be okay anyway. Hope that *four* hadn't been just a fluke.

# Chapter 4

Hurrying out of Geography the following Thursday afternoon, I smacked into Carl Smythe, Jerry's younger brother. Carl was only fifteen; he was starting ninth grade for the second time, biding his time until his sixteenth birthday would set him free from the prison he called school.

"Hey, Tee-baby," he sneered. "Looks like you don't watch where you're walking either. Speaking of near-sighted morons, how is your veggie father?"

I ignored him, kept walking, made a beeline for the Chemistry lab down the hall.

"Shut up, Carl," his girlfriend Missy said.

"I'm not going to shut up. You shut up, bitch. My big brother's in the joint because her asshole father is a jaywalker."

That was going to be Jerry's stupid defence, I'd heard. That Mel had been so absorbed in his coffee and bagel that morning he'd stepped off the sidewalk into the path of Jerry's car. Jerry's lawyer didn't seem to care that at least three credible witnesses saw the souped-up red Camaro jump the curb.

I could feel Carl getting closer, his hot, sour breath on my neck. "I heard your smarty-pants father's got the I.Q. of a turnip now," he cackled.

I kept on walking, past the Chemistry room. There was a washroom near the end of the hall. I was suddenly feeling sick. My eyes burned, but damn him if anyone was going to see me cry.

"Come on, Carl," Missy whined. "Let's have a smoke before class." Smoking wasn't allowed on school property, not that it bothered people like Carl and Missy, who begged to be expelled.

Carl stopped walking, but yelled after me, "Hey, do you have to change your daddy's diapers or is there a nurse to do it?"

His evil laughter echoed in my ears as I passed the bathroom, ran down a flight of stairs, and pushed through the double doors to the deserted sports field. I was due in Chemistry. Ethan and I had a major class project to work on. But I knew I wouldn't be making it to class. Not that day. I'm sorry, Mr. Harnett, I thought. Please don't take it personally.

I made it across the field to the trees behind the bleachers before the sobs began.

"Tee!" I heard Ethan shout from about twenty metres behind me. "Tee, wait up!"

I kept running, down the wooded trail that led to Riverside Park. I'm a pretty good distance runner, could probably manage 10k if I paced myself, even in the leather Tevas I'd worn that day. I didn't expect Ethan to be able to keep up for long.

I was wrong.

Ethan ran up alongside me. "Please stop, Tee. I want to talk."

"No," I gasped and tried to go faster.

"Please." Ethan grabbed my arm, gently but firmly, and wouldn't let go.

I stopped. "Let go, Ethan," I sniffed.

He let go. "Let me help."

I rolled my eyes. "You can't help. No one can help."

"Well, I can listen."

"What good is that? It won't make my father feel better."

Ethan looked me in the eye. "It might make you feel better."

"Just leave me alone."

Ethan ignored that. "Tee, I told you about my sister. I don't know what happened to your father, but I do know what it's like to be worried, *crazy-worried*, about a family member. You can talk to me, Tee."

"I can't," I sighed.

"You can," Ethan repeated. "You don't scare me."

"I scare everyone else."

Ethan looked perplexed. "Why is that, Tee? About twenty kids heard what went on upstairs with you and that jackass—Carl's his name? Twenty kids I'm sure you've known since kindergarten. Why was I the only one who followed you out here?"

I just stood there shaking. "Please, go away," I whimpered.

Instead, Ethan took three steps forward and enveloped me in his sweatshirt.

I didn't push him away. He smelled like homemade chocolate chip cookies. "If you stay and talk to me, you're going to miss Chemistry," I said into his shoulder. I'm tall, five-eight, and Ethan was at least six inches taller.

"I can't get anything done without you there anyway, partner," he lied. "We can get the assignment from Mr. Harnett after class and work on it at home. Tomorrow, maybe? I've probably got the stuff we need at my place."

I shook my head. "Tomorrow I'm seeing my dad in the morning, then driving to Toronto for the weekend. It was my mom's birthday last week and I haven't visited all summer. "

I could imagine Ethan's wheels turning, trying to figure out my complicated family dynamics from what little I'd given him. "How about tonight, then?" he asked. "My parents are going to some CF parent group and I'm babysitting. Ellie's old enough to stay out of our way. Say around seven?"

"I guess. Okay." I tried to smile but knew I looked terrible with my eyes all red and puffy, my nose dripping.

"Glad that's settled. Now," Ethan added, grabbing my hand, "where can we go to talk?"

I led him a little farther along the park trail to the Witch's Tree.

"The Witch's Tree?" Ethan asked.

I explained, "On windy days, the lower branches sway in a way that some people think looks like the long, gnarled arms of a witch beckoning to passers by. It's spooky at night." I paused. "Last spring, my dad and I jogged through here every night before dinner."

"Tee?"

I sighed. "Ethan, what have you already heard? You've been here almost two weeks, and I know how fast gossip orbits through the cafeteria."

Ethan shrugged. "I haven't heard much, really; I've been spending a lot of lunch hours in the library. I did over-hear two girls talking one day about another girl whose name I didn't catch. Something about her father being hit by a car and no one knowing if he'd regain his memory or be permanently brain damaged. They said that the girl had a nervous breakdown of something, hadn't spoken to any of her friends over the summer, refused to live with her mother in Toronto.

"I figured it was you the day I drove you home. Stuff you said about your dad being away, you living with your aunt. Then there's the way most people avoid you when they can. And they're so polite, *too polite*, when they can't. There's there's this guy who sits behind me in Economics— Joey. He asked me a few days ago how you were; I guess he'd seen the two of us talking by our lockers. I asked him why he didn't ask you himself, but he just shrugged."

"Joey and I used to date last spring," I sighed. "He dumped me three days before the end of school. My dad's accident happened a week later. Joey left me a bunch of phone messages over the summer—lots of kids did—but I didn't feel like talking to anyone. My whole summer was consumed with visiting my dad every evening and working days at a science camp in Ottawa. The job was great; no one knew me. It took a bit of pressure off; I could just pretend everything was fine."

"You still see your dad every day?"

I shook my head. "Aunt George goes two afternoons a week and insisted I cut back to just Saturdays. I fought her on it, but she won by convincing me how upset Mel would be if he knew I was jeopardizing my chances of getting into a good university by visiting him every night instead of studying. It's too bad I really *do* want to go to university," I laughed. "If I wanted to drop out of high school and become a street musician, Mel wouldn't put up much of an argument the way he is right now."

Ethan was quiet. "You're a lot like me."

"In what way?"

"You make jokes to hide what you're really thinking."

"Beats slitting my wrists, I guess," I said.

Ethan's eyes grew wide. "You haven't tried that, have you?"

I shook my head. "If I wanted to commit suicide, I'd use pills. I'd hate to stain Aunt George's expensive bathroom tiles."

"Tee?"

"Sorry. Just another bad attempt at levity."

"What really happened, Tee?"

"To my dad?"

"To you, too."

Ethan was still holding my hand, looking at me with curious and non-judgmental eyes, wanting to know my story. His skin was dry and warm and rough with calluses the way a hard-working rural kid's should be. What would his girlfriend think if she knew Ethan was holding another girl's hand? I knew he meant to be supportive, not romantic, but still I wondered what the deal really was between them.

Since Ethan showed no signs of giving up on me, I told him everything. How it had been Carl's older brother, Jerry, at the wheel. How I'd seemingly become Carl's "special project" since that day. I told him everything I knew about Mel's accident. How the strong and intelligent man Mel had been seemed lost now inside his injured brain. I told him about my mother, why she lived in Toronto now, how our relationship had always been strained. And about the kids at school who knew me as a brain and an athlete, a happy kid who'd come through her parent's divorce seemingly unscathed. How they'd never met the mess I became without my father's love and guidance. And how they'd become wary of this angry, confused girl who now knew way too much about the fragility of the human body.

"I think my father's improving, at least a little," I added, embarrassed to be caught wallowing in self-pity. "Mel is getting stronger; he can bear weight on his legs and has started taking steps with a walker. He's talking more, even though most of what he says doesn't make sense. He feeds himself pudding and mashed potatoes, sticky stuff that doesn't fall off the spoon too easily. He can count and read a little, first grade stuff, but I've been reading him more advanced books, Hardy Boys and whatever. He's not ready for *War and Peace*."

"It's a good start," Ethan said.

I shrugged. "His memory is still bad. I'm so terrified he may never remember who he is, what he was, who I am, his family. The doctors keep saying 'give it time,' but it hurts so much that he doesn't remember me." I started blubbering again.

"Ethan?" I sniffed, feeling ridiculous, but powerless to stop the flow of tears. "I'm not usually such a crybaby."

"I figured that," Ethan grinned. "You should do this more often. Cry. You said it yourself—the kids here, your old friends, anyway, have never seen your vulnerability. You only show them what you want them to see—your strengths."

I was guilty as charged. Even when Joey dumped me, I'd been a good sport about it, told him I understood when I didn't, saved my tears and anguish for behind my closed bedroom door.

"Well, congratulations. You've just seen my so-called vulnerability," I said. "And then some."

"Good. Now I don't have to be afraid to show you mine," Ethan grinned.

"You? Vulnerable?" I knew Ethan's life wasn't problem free—it was quite the contrary by the sounds of it. But he seemed so confident, so good-humoured, so damn *wise*. Or was that merely what *he'd* chosen to show *me*?

"For starters," he said, pointing to his green wire frames. "I'm not just nearsighted; I'm colour-blind. My mom still picks out my clothes in the morning."

I grinned. "So *that's* why you need my help in Chemistry. All Mr. Harnett's charts are colour-coded."

In the distance, the dismissal bell rang.

"We'd better get back if we want to talk to Mr. Harnett about a make-up assignment," Ethan said, dropping my hand at last.

"What will we tell him?" I asked, standing and brushing tree bark from my jeans.

"That I had diarrhea," Ethan laughed. "And since I'm the new kid, you were kind enough to show me the way to the pharmacy so I could buy a bottle of Kaopectate. I doubt he'll press for details."

Turned out Ethan and I didn't have to say anything. We ran into Mr. Harnett on the stairwell on our way back into the school building.

"Hey, you two," he said, beckoning us to the landing. "Everything okay?" He flashed me a look of concern and raised a brow at Ethan.

"Yes, sir," I nodded.

Mr. Harnett rummaged in his briefcase. "I was hoping to run into the two of you. Take these." He handed Ethan and me stapled packages containing the assignment we'd missed and photocopies of his class notes. "Your assignment's due by Wednesday."

"Thank you, sir," I said, surprised at his generosity. Mr. Harnett was known as a bit of a hard-ass when it came to missed classes. He must know what happened, I realized, feeling embarrassed.

"We haven't really met," Mr. Harnett said to Ethan, shaking his hand. "But what I've seen so far is commendable." I knew Mr. Harnett wasn't referring just to Ethan's smarts.

Then he turned to me. "Could I talk to you privately for a few minutes, Theresa?"

Ethan waved and said he'd expect me around seven. He'd offered me a ride home, but I had the Jeep. Although the bus strike was over, it made no sense to waste an hour each morning and afternoon on a smelly, noisy, sardine can of a school bus when I had the Jeep and Mel's gas card at my disposal. Because of Mel's incapacity, Aunt George had been granted temporary power of attorney over his finances. With her zillions, I knew she'd never take money from Mel's disability cheques or the rent income from the house to provide room and board for me. Instead, she told me to buy whatever I needed with Mel's credit cards and give her the bills when they arrived. The gas was my only real extravagance. I hadn't had the time or inclination to become a shopaholic.

When we were alone on the landing, Mr. Harnett spoke. "Your dad's my best friend. You know that, Theresa."

I nodded.

He continued, "Ordinarily you'd be in deep trouble for skipping, but Joey told me what happened in the hall before class today. I know you two are on the outs—his fault, he admits—but it seems he still cares about you as a friend. And," he added, "Just so you know, Carl's left the school, probably for good. I can't give you the details, but I think he's one person you won't need to worry about anymore."

My relief overwhelmed my curiosity. I let out a huge breath.

"You've still got friends, Theresa. They're young and don't always know how to say what they feel or do the right thing, and to be perfectly blunt, you haven't exactly been receptive to their fumbled attempts to connect with you. I know that sometimes it's easier to talk to a new friend than your old ones."

I shrugged. Sometimes it was easier not to talk at all.

"Mr. Stinson will make a good lab partner—there's chemistry between you." Mr. Harnett laughed at his own pun and then changed the subject. "I saw Mel yesterday."

Mr. Harnett coached a Wednesday night peewee basketball team at the Ottawa Boys and Girls Club. He visited Mel before each week's practice.

"How was he?" I asked.

"Great. Very alert."

I lit up. "Did he remember something while you were there?"

"Remember? No, but he was reading Harry Potter to me. It was slow going—he needed to follow along with his finger—but the words are coming back, Theresa, even the long ones."

"That's great," I said, with perhaps nowhere near as much enthusiasm as the situation warranted. Dr. Seuss to Harry Potter in four days was really quite a leap.

Mr. Harnett frowned. "I know you *want* him to remember, Theresa. I know how hard it is for me, so I can only imagine how much harder it is for you to deal with the fact he can't remember his family and friends. But he's getting to know you and your aunt and me again. It's not the same, I know. Starting from scratch never is. But he thinks about you when you aren't there. By the way, he wants more oatmeal raisin cookies the next time you visit."

"Huh? I've never brought Mel any cookies."

"That's odd. He said you make, I quote, 'really yummy oatmeal raisin cookies.' And you know what a mouthful that was for him to enunciate."

I nodded. "It's just, I haven't made cookies in months. Not since way before."

Mr. Harnett was jubilant. "See, he remembered your cookies!"

"Oh joy," I smirked. "Tee the Weekend Visitor has been promoted to Tee the Cookie Monster."

Mr. Harnett was frustrated by my sarcasm. "Theresa, be patient. I'm not going to patronize you and tell you everything is going to be just fine. But things are improving. Physically Mel is progressing faster than anyone anticipated. His speech is still delayed, but he rarely speaks gibberish anymore. The doctor said many brain-injured patients get depressed or agitated, but Mel is in pretty good spirits, all things considered. I think he knows on some level that he has good reasons to work hard at the therapy, that he has good work and good people and a good life to get back to."

I nodded again. "I'm seeing him tomorrow. I'll make some cookies."

"Make some for me, too."

"Is that a homework assignment?"

"Call it extra credit," Mr. Harnett grinned.

"Why's that?"

"You're brilliant, Theresa. Brilliant enough to know that Mr. Stinson is the only serious competition you have in the race for valedictorian. You know it's based entirely on senior level marks."

I rolled my eyes. "I don't care about being valedictorian." Truth was I hated public speaking. The poignancy of any speech I wrote would be lost the moment I reached the podium and gracelessly wet my pants.

"Mel cares."

"Mel *cared*," I corrected.

"Mel will care again, Theresa. Mark my words. Have a good weekend. Don't you and Ethan study too hard," Mr. Harnett winked.

Cookies, I thought on my way to the Jeep. I need to make cookies.

# Chapter 5

Aunt George was picking weeds in the front garden when I arrived home an hour later carrying three bulging bags of baking ingredients. She straightened up to her full six feet and brushed dirt off her knees.

"Home Ec. project?" she asked.

"No. I'm baking cookies. Mr. Harnett claims Mel asked for some of my oatmeal raisin cookies last night."

Aunt George nodded and smiled, "It seems every day now he's remembering something. I visited this morning so you'd have him to yourself tomorrow. Mel asked about the 'big puppy.'"

I raised a brow. "He remembered Harley? But you'd only had her a week before—"

"I know." Aunt George grinned.

"Maybe he'll remember *me* tomorrow," I said excitedly. "Maybe the cookies will remind him how I set the oven on fire the first time I made them trying to get my Brownie cooking badge."

Aunt George laughed. "Wouldn't it be spectacular if he could get back all his good memories, but not his bad ones?"

I grinned. "Like if he permanently forgot the time I accidentally hot-washed all his lab coats in the same load as my red hockey uniform?"

Aunt George grew wistful. "But you know, Theresa, it's the good *and* bad memories that make us who we are, teach us how to cope, let us grow."

"Do you think Mel remembers what happened?" I asked.

Aunt George shook her head. "No. He's been *told* he was hit by a car, that the driver lost control and drove over the sidewalk. He's been *told* I'm his sister and you're his daughter and Ron Harnett is his friend, but it's hard for him to understand the complexities of formal relationships when he doesn't have memories to draw from. He's remembering simple things right now: cookies, puppies."

"He remembered Lucy's birthday."

"True."

"And he figured out my algebra problem."

"Maybe. The therapist said to try another on him tomorrow or next week."

"Are there cases of people gaining back all their previous knowledge without gaining back their memories?" I asked.

Aunt George pondered. "Yes, I think it's possible. Even if Mel doesn't regain his memory, the occupational therapist thinks he may gain back enough skills and knowledge to work again. Maybe not teaching, but..." Aunt George didn't want to think about it either. Teaching was Mel's life, his old life, anyway.

But at least people were starting to talk about Mel's long-term future like he might actually have one. I knew that even if Mel spent the next forty years in bed eating Cheetos and reading Harry Potter, even if he didn't know he was my father, I'd stick with him, adjusting my own future plans to make sure he always had someone nearby who loved him and who could look after his best interests. It was the least I could do.

I glanced at my watch. "I better get started on the cookies," I said. "Ethan and I are getting together after dinner to finish a Chemistry assignment." I was hesitant about telling Aunt George why we were behind. She had enough to worry about without knowing I was being harrassed at school.

"You two got something sizzling on the Bunsen burner?" she laughed.

I rolled my eyes in exasperation. "We're just lab partners."

"All the better to experiment with, my dear."

"One of these days I'm going to put rat poison in your Metamucil," I joked.

"Hey, I like that. I can use it in my next book."

"What will you title it? *The Constipated Corpse*?"

Aunt George laughed and waved me off. "If you want something besides cookies for dinner, you can nuke the left-over casserole that's in the fridge. I want to flesh out a few pages in the office when I'm finished here. I'll make a sandwich for myself later, after you've left for your date, oops, study session."

The old Harper place was as I remembered it: a big weathered farmhouse, a small barn, and two aluminium equipment sheds. A narrow field extended beyond the sheds to a dense lot of silver birch and sugar maples. Beyond the trees, the river surged towards nearby rapids.

I arrived at the front door carrying my chemistry text-book and a shoebox bulging with cookies.

"Hey, you didn't have to bring cookies," Ethan said, biting into one. "But I'm glad you did. Thanks," he added with his mouth full.

I'd made six dozen. There was a huge tin at home to bring to Mel in the morning and a smaller tin stashed in the freezer for Mr. Harnett. I knew he'd only been teasing about the cookies for extra credit, but he was a good guy and I'd smuggle them into his briefcase anyway as a joke.

"Thank you for this afternoon, Ethan. I feel a lot better about things."

"At your service, Miss Tee," Ethan grinned. "Come on in."

The Stinson's new home was warm and newly painted in creams and taupes. The hardwood floors were worn but freshly varnished. The furniture looked put-up-your-feet comfortable. Open boxes were piled everywhere.

"Sorry about the mess," Ethan said. "I cleared a space for us to work at the kitchen table." He steered me down a short hallway.

"This is my sister, Ellie." Ethan pointed to a tall, waifish girl washing dinner dishes in the sink.

"Hi." She turned and gave me a wave of her yellow rubber glove.

"You going to be through with the cleanup soon, servant girl?" Ethan asked.

Ellie flicked soap at him. "If you didn't eat so much, there wouldn't be so many dishes."

"If you hadn't lost the last round of poker, I'd have had them done long ago."

I laughed. "You decide who does dishes by playing poker?"

Ellie raised a brow. "Of course. How do you do it at your house?"

"She has a dishwasher," Ethan answered for me. "Where are Ernie and Bert?"

"Up in my room," Ellie replied. "I figured you wouldn't want them chewing on your smelly sneakers while you studied."

"Come with me." Ethan gestured for me to follow him up the stairs.

"Price of admission just went up, big brother!" Ellie shouted.

Ethan explained, "She charges me a dollar any time I go into her room uninvited."

"And don't think about cutting a two-for-one deal!" Ellie shouted again.

Ethan opened a bright purple door at the end of the upstairs hall and stood back while two furball puppies swarmed me. They were tiny retrievers, straw-coloured, and probably not more than eight-weeks-old.

"Hey, babies!" I crouched down on the floor and let them crawl over me and gnaw my sleeves with their sharp little puppy teeth.

I loved animals both wild and domestic, but I hadn't mentioned to Ethan my dreams of becoming a zoologist. There didn't seem to be much point, since the path of my future would now be determined by the speed and extent of Mel's recovery. I'd even busted my butt the previous year taking extra evening courses so I'd have enough credits to apply to a special program at a B.C. university that allows eligible high school seniors to begin under-graduate studies in January.

At the time, Mel and I had been excited about the possibility of me getting a head start on my post-secondary education, but now, without a miracle, it looked like I'd be firmly anchored in North Creek come January. I could volunteer at the local animal shelter, spend more time with Mel, apply to universities closer to home, and then head off with my peers next September. Maybe things would be better by then, or at least more settled. Or not.

"You okay?" Ethan asked, taking note of my spaced-out

expression.

"Yeah. Sorry. Which is which?" I gestured to the puppies.

"Ernie has the wider forehead, Bert has the longer muzzle," Ethan explained. "They're brothers. Some lady from down the road came by with them yesterday and offered them as a housewarming gift. Typical story: her sweet, innocent Golden got knocked up by the badass Lab next door. There were eleven pups altogether; she'd managed to find homes for the other nine. My parents think we've got enough to do right now without housebreaking puppies, but Ellie fell in love and Dad figures they'll take her mind off getting a horse, which he knows we can't afford unless he wins the lottery."

A phone rang in the kitchen.

Seconds later, Ellie appeared in the doorway carrying a cordless. "Ethan, it's Tina."

"Tell her I'm busy," Ethan whispered. "I'll call her tomorrow."

"She'll be mad," Ellie said in a singsong voice, covering the mouthpiece with her hand. "Especially if I tell her..." She cocked her head at me.

Ethan gave Ellie a look that would freeze molten lava. "Just tell her I'll call tomorrow."

"He's busy right now," Ellie said into the phone, barely suppressing a giggle. "He's been in the bathroom for over an hour. ...Something he ate, I think....By the sounds of it, it's *both* ends....If he lives, he'll call you tomorrow."

I thought he'd be furious, but Ethan laughed. "See? The gastrointestinal excuse works every time."

"I'm finished in the kitchen," Ellie announced, putting the cordless in the pocket of her sweater and scooping up the puppies. "Time to venture out for a leak, boys. Oh—"

She looked up at me. "In case you're wondering, it's Ethan who's adopted, not me." Ellie turned and clomped down the stairs, her words hanging in the air.

Truthfully, I had been wondering. There was no denying Ellie's Asian features.

Ethan laughed. "Ellie's nose is a little out of joint, today. She brought home some girls from school to see the puppies. Mom and Dad had already left for the city. When the girls met me, Ellie's big *blond* brother, one girl confided to Ellie that her parents were thinking of adopting a Chinese orphan, too."

"Ouch," I said.

Ethan continued. "Ellie's half *South Korean*, on Mom's side. Dad's Irish. We're all Newfoundlanders first and foremost. My biological parents were French-Canadian oceanographers who died in a storm off the Grand Banks when I was three. The Stinsons were their best friends and next-door neighbours; I usually stayed with them when my parents were away at sea. That last time I just stayed for good. My grandparents kept in touch over the years, but they're gone now, too."

"Do you remember your biological parents?" I asked.

Ethan shook his head. "I have photographs, but no clear memories of being with them. Sometimes I get fuzzy flashes of me sitting on the shoulders of a red-haired man at a Santa Claus parade—my biological father had red hair—but that's it. Maybe it's easier I don't remember. Easier to accept the Stinsons as my parents. Easier not to miss them."

"Do you think you just don't want to remember?" I asked, staring out Ellie's bedroom window into the twilight.

Ethan shook his head. "No, Dr. Phil. I think I was just too young to remember. I know what you're thinking, Tee. That maybe your Dad does remember you but he's blocking it intentionally, that it's too painful for him to deal with memories of a rich life he may not get back. That it's enough of a challenge just learning to put one foot in front of the other again."

I shrugged.

"But I think you're wrong, Tee," Ethan continued. "I think when he's got it in him to remember, he will. From what you've told me, your dad loves you too much to hold you at arms length if he could hold you closer, even if it is painful for him. If you don't give up on him, Tee, he won't give up on himself. Give his brain time to heal."

"Who sounds like Dr. Phil now?"

Ethan pointed me back towards the kitchen. "We'd better get to work."

Two hours later, we were tying up the last chemistry problem when Ellie came out of the bathroom and shuffled into the kitchen wearing huge bunny slippers and a faded pink housecoat with a drooping hem.

"Did you take your pills?" Ethan asked her.

A nod.

"Finish your Ensure shake?"

Ellie made a face and nodded. "Mask and thumps are done, too."

"Are the puppies in their crate?"

Another nod.

"Then hit the sack, kid," Ethan said. "Tee and I are almost done here. I'll be up in a while."

Ellie hesitated, glancing over at me. "Ethan, can you drive me into town? I have to buy something."

Ethan balked. "Are you crazy? It's late. You're in your

pajamas, for Pete's sake!"

Ellie looked desperate. "So I'll get dressed. It's important. Mom won't be home for hours."

"Are you sick?" Ethan asked, clearly skeptical.

"I don't think so, but…"

"Then scram."

"I got…" Ellie mumbled something I didn't hear.

"What?"

"I…." Ellie looked almost in tears. She mumbled something else.

Ethan was exasperated. *"Ellie, what do you want!"*

*"I GOT MY PERIOD!"* she yelled, her olive skin now rosy with embarrassment.

There was a long pause. "So?" Ethan said finally.

Ellie started to cry in earnest. "There's no…" She didn't finish the sentence. Instead, she stomped her foot on the floor and slammed back into the bathroom.

Ethan looked at me and shrugged.

"And to think I had you pegged as Mr. Sensitive." I shook my head. "Has she had it before?"

"Had what?"

"Her period, you idiot!" I rolled my eyes in disgust.

Ethan shrugged again, but stood up. "Maybe I should…"

I motioned for him to sit back down. "You finish the homework. Let me handle this," I said, grabbing my backpack and making a beeline for the bathroom door.

"Hey, Ellie," I called. I could hear raspy sobs coming from within.

"Go away!"

"Open up. I have what you need in my pack. Enough to hold you over until your mother or—" I glared back at Ethan, "—your *grossly insensitive* brother can take you to the store tomorrow."

Ellie opened the door a crack.

I grinned at her, glad that I would never have to be twelve again. "I've been getting my period for years, Ellie. I'm a professional. Let me help."

Ellie opened the door and motioned for me to come in. She shut the door and locked it behind us. "I'm sorry," she sniffed. "My mom usually keeps her stuff in the cabinet under the sink, but look." Ellie held an empty box upside down. "None left. She must have run out. I'm sorry I cried; I must sound like a baby, but I've never done this before. My brother is such an asshole sometimes."

"Guys say dumb stuff when they're embarrassed."

Ellie gasped. "*He's* embarrassed? What about me? Ethan hates me."

"I doubt it."

"It's my lousy fault we moved here. He had to leave his dumb girlfriend back in Newfoundland."

"I don't think he blames you." I dug around in my backpack and pulled out the trial-size box of tampons I carried around as insurance against being caught off guard. "Can you manage these? You know how they work?"

Ellie nodded. "I think so. Back home, last summer, my friend Melanie and I practiced with some we stole from her sister."

"That's the spirit," I laughed. "I'll leave you alone, then. Call me back if there's a problem."

"Can I ask you a question before you go? My mom's not real comfortable talking about sex and, well, you saw how Ethan is with girly stuff."

"Give it a whirl," I said, not bothering to inform her I was hardly the voice of experience.

Ellie took a deep breath. "Can I get pregnant now?"

"Not if you don't have sex," I replied.

"Is twelve too young for sex?"

"Yes." Call me old-fashioned, *but*.

Ellie raised a brow. "There's a girl in my class at school who said she's done it lots of times."

I laughed. "She's probably lying, and if she isn't, she shouldn't be bragging about it."

"Have you?" Ellie asked.

It crossed my mind that I should probably just tell her to mind her own business, but there was nothing judgmental in her question, only curiosity. I shook my head. Joey had wanted to from practically our first date. He'd never pushed me to do more than I wanted, but I always knew it was only a matter of time before we either closed the deal or broke up.

"Ethan was sleeping with Tina back in Newfoundland," Ellie whispered.

I smirked. "How do you know?"

"I saw them once by accident; they were going at it in the basement rec room and didn't hear me on the stairs. Ethan thought I was riding my bike outside. I won't bore you with the gross details."

"Gee, thanks."

"Anyway, it's not like I stuck around and *watched*," Ellie said. "Ethan's going back to Newfoundland to spend Thanksgiving with Tina and her family; she gave him the plane ticket as a going-away present. But I hope they break up; she's *so* annoying."

"Let's change the subject." I had no idea how much sound carried through the bathroom door and I didn't want to take the chance that Ethan could hear us talking about him.

"Okay," Ellie said, and then asked, "Do you want to have kids someday?"

Good question. "Maybe. When I'm older, finished

university, have an exciting job."

"I don't want to have babies ever." Ellie was vehement.

"No?"

"Ethan told you I have cystic fibrosis, right?"

I nodded.

"It's a recessive genetic disorder. You must know what that means if you were willing to work with Einstein out there. My parents are both carriers. There was a one in four chance I'd inherit their two normal genes and be, well, normal. There was a fifty per cent chance I'd inherit one CF gene and one normal gene and be a carrier like my parents; lots of kids are and don't even know it. But I lucked out and got the two CF genes," Ellie sighed. "If I had kids, even with a normal guy, they'd automatically be carriers. If they had kids with another carrier, their kids could end up like me. And I wouldn't wish CF on anybody."

I raised my eyebrows. This was high school biology; Ellie knew her stuff. "Can't carriers be tested?"

Ellie nodded. "But genetics aside, even if my kids were fine, I'd make a bad parent...being sick all the time." She suddenly sounded so old for her years, like she spent many hours thinking about the mysteries of life and her own mortality.

"You seem okay now," I said. True, she was too thin and coughed like a chain-smoker, but she was far from bedridden. And hadn't Ethan said some CF kids were living into middle adulthood?

Ellie shrugged. "It's an illusion. You haven't seen the cabinet full of drugs I take each day to keep me 'seeming okay.' Average life expectancy for a CF kid right now is about thirty-five. Mild cases last longest. More severe cases, well..."

"You're mild, right?" I asked hopefully.

She shook her head. "Mine's pretty bad," Ellie confided, then gave a raspy laugh. "I could go at any time. I better get to work here," she added, waving the box of tampons and tossing off my look of concern. "Thanks for the help."

Ethan shot me a wary look as I headed back to the kitchen table. "I finished writing up the last results. Thanks for...you know." He nodded towards the bathroom door.

"No problem. Go easy on her; she might be a little crampy."

"You were in there a long time."

"Girl talk," I grinned. "She wanted to know if twelve was too young for sex."

Ethan gasped. "What did you tell her?"

"That it was okay as long as she really loved the boy."

*"WHAT?"*

I laughed. "I advised against it. She also told me she thinks you hate her."

"Why? Just because I wouldn't drive her to the store?" Ethan was genuinely shocked.

"Because you had to leave your girlfriend when you moved here."

Ethan shook his head. "I didn't have to. I could have stayed at my buddy Rob's house if I'd wanted."

"Then why did you come?"

"They're my family. I love them. Tina and I would have been separated when I went to university, anyway. If we can't make it apart now, we probably can't make it apart a year from now, either," Ethan shrugged.

"Ethan, I know this is none of my business, but why didn't you take Tina's call? You could have gone into another room, had privacy. I hope you didn't blow her off on my account."

Ellie came out of the bathroom and gave me the thumbs up. She stuck her tongue out at Ethan. "Nighty night, slug," she yawned, setting off up the stairs to her room.

"I'm sorry, El," he called.

Ellie laughed and called back, "So am I. I just scrubbed the toilet with your toothbrush."

Ethan groaned and said to me, "Where were we?"

"Trouble in paradise."

He hesitated.

"I'm sorry, Ethan. I don't want to pry. I shouldn't have said anything."

Ethan shook his head. "No, it's okay, it's good. Maybe what I need is a different female perspective. It's just hard for me to admit Tina and I are having problems."

"You must miss her so much."

"That's just it, I don't. Or not as much as I thought I would, anyway. And lately when she calls, we end up fighting. She spends money she doesn't have calling me twice, sometimes three times a day, just to check up on me. She drills me on every single thing I'm doing, why I'm doing it, who I'm doing it with. It's like she's upset because I'm starting to enjoy it here. I mean, the kids are friendly, the teachers know how to challenge me, I'm starting a good-paying weekend job next week splitting logs and mucking stalls at the big Rainson farm down the road. I don't want to feel guilty because I'm not angry and depressed and wishing I could go back to Newfoundland. I've been away less than a month. How could she have changed so fast? Why the *Fatal Attraction* theatrics?"

I shrugged. "Maybe it's you who's changed."

"Nah." Ethan shook his head.

I didn't want to argue. "What's she like? Tina?"

Ethan's eyes lit up. "Cute. Short. Plays clarinet in the

school band. Works after school at her father's hardware store."

"How did you hook up?"

Ethan chewed on his lip. "Tina was having trouble with Biology and English last fall and needed a peer tutor or risked getting tossed from the band. I started meeting her at the library every day after school. She passed her midterms and I asked her to the Christmas dance at the Y. We started dating. Then just when things started getting serious, I found out about the move. Tina was pretty upset. She had this whole future thing worked out for us; I'd go to university, she'd work and save money, we'd buy a house, get married, live happily ever after."

I cringed. "Were you okay with the 'whole future thing'?"

"I wasn't *not* okay with it, I just couldn't relate to it, to be honest. Maybe it's not cool to admit this, but Tina is my first girlfriend. I love being with her, but I'm not ready to even *think* about marriage, let alone shop for the damn promise ring she was hinting at before I left. She's only sixteen, but in her family, all the older sisters were married and had kids before they were twenty."

I winced. "I can't imagine being married for years, if ever. At least thirty. I want to study, travel, make sure my father is taken care of. Don't get me wrong; I like guys as much as the next girl, but my life has too many variables right now to plan what I'll do next week, let alone for the rest of my life."

"So you do understand. You don't think I'm being a terrible and selfish boyfriend for wanting, for *enjoying*, a bit of time and space?"

"Definitely not," I said, but I couldn't help but wonder how I'd feel if I were Tina. If Ethan were my boyfriend, would I feel comfortable with him getting chummy and sharing his troubles with another girl? Not likely.

"My Aunt George thinks long distance love is too much work. She was married to a travelling salesman."

Ethan nodded. "I considered making a clean break—thought it would be better for both of us. But Tina cried and said how much she loved me and that she'd wait for me and, well, it got to me. You have to understand that before Tina, girls never paid me any attention—not that way."

"Why not?"

Ethan raised a brow. "Haven't you noticed? I'm a geek, Tee, even by small town standards."

"Define 'geek.'"

"I think math and science are fun. I suck at team sports. I couldn't see you across the table without my glasses. My mom has to pick out my school clothes…"

"Is *that* all?" I laughed.

Ethan sighed and pulled back his thick shoulder-length hair. "I'm not trying to look like a cocker spaniel, but my ears stick out like Mr. Spock from the old Star Trek shows—I have to keep them covered. Before Tina, girls, when they thought of me at all, considered me as just 'guy-friend' material."

"Ethan?" I asked. "May I be honest?"

"Fire away."

"It's a *gift* to be as good at math and science as you are—you have what it takes to be the Bill Gates of DNA. And you may suck at team sports, and I know it's a big deal at North Creek, but you keep fit somehow." I reached across the table and squeezed his arm. "You don't get biceps like this working math problems."

Ethan shrugged. "Farm work."

I continued, "Your mom does a commendable job

choosing clothes that pass for normal—this is North Creek, after all, not Paris. And okay, your ears are pointy and stick out a little, but you're hardly a Vulcan. Ethan?"

He blushed. "I'm not sure I want to hear anymore of this."

"You're fit, smart, and funny. And you were a great 'guy friend' to me when I really needed one. In my dictionary, that doesn't spell 'geek.'" I gathered my books together and grabbed my jacket from behind the chair.

"What does it spell?"

"Sexy." I glanced at the clock over the stove. It was almost eleven. "I'd better run."

Ethan followed me to the door, opened it, and laughed. "I can't believe you just said that."

I punched him on the shoulder. "I can't believe you fell for it. See you in school Monday."

# Chapter 6

On my way to visit Mel the next morning I stopped at the Esso self-serve on Foster's Mill Road. I'd been going out of my way to gas up at the Petro-Canada on the highway for the past three months, but it was now time to face the music. I needed something besides gas that morning.

The morning rush was over and Joey was at the counter in the convenience store reading a *Penthouse* he'd pilfered from the magazine rack.

"Hey, Joey." I laid a twenty on the counter to cover the gas. "I took a chance you'd be here today."

Joey set the magazine down and put the twenty in the till. "You're looking good, Tee."

I had made a better than average effort that morning: off-white cotton pants instead of jeans; the taupe sweater Lucy had given me for my birthday back in May that she said brought out the gold flecks in my brown eyes; a suede hair band to hold back my thick, straight hair instead of the twisted bandana I usually wore when I bothered to pull my hair back at all; and quick swipes of mascara and lipgloss. I didn't want to overdo it; Mel might not recognize me as Tee the Weekend Visitor or otherwise, but Lucy would be impressed, which was the point. She wouldn't feel inclined to spend the weekend dragging me through Winners or the Eaton Centre.

"Thanks, Joey," I said. "Thanks also for talking to Mr. Harnett yesterday when I ditched Chemistry. I know I should have stood up to that pond scum Carl, but I just…" I didn't know what else to say.

"You don't have to explain," Joey said. "Carl's an asshole; everyone knows it but him. I could see you were on the verge of a meltdown yesterday, Tee. I would have gone after you myself, but Newfie-boy beat me to it."

I wasn't so sure about that, but I let it go. "I talked to Mr. Harnett later in the afternoon," I said. "He told me Carl left school and wouldn't be back."

Joey nodded. "Missy reported him."

"His girlfriend? Reported him for what?"

"You haven't heard? For selling drugs. It was all everyone was talking about in town last night. Scoop is Missy asked to be excused from Family Studies to use the washroom and dashed to the office instead. She slipped Principal Magee the number of Carl's non-regulation lock, told him Carl was playing pharmacist at his locker every morning before homeroom, and tipped him off that Carl kept his stash in a hollowed-out French-English dictionary on the top shelf."

I was confused. "Why? Why did she do it?"

"Carl and Missy have been on the outs for a while; rumour is he started slapping her around over the summer and she was biding her time for an opportunity to bring him down without getting her teeth knocked out in the process. And don't you remember that her brother Steve was in that car full of students coming back from the Grad a few years ago?"

"Refresh me."

"The driver was drinking beer at the wheel and drove right into the side of a train at Barr's Crossing. Steve was the only one to survive the crash. He lost both legs and an eye.

Died of a painkiller overdose six month's later. Missy's not the sharpest tack on the corkboard, Tee, but she knows drinking and driving isn't something to make jokes or tease someone about."

"Isn't Missy afraid that Carl will come after her when he's let off?" I asked. "He's not one to forget an insult."

Joey shrugged. "I heard she's planning to hitchhike to Halifax; her father lives there. And now that he's been nailed for selling, Carl will be in closed custody for awhile. His mom signed him over to Children's Aid last night; even she's had enough of him."

I was astounded. "All this happened because Carl harrassed me about Mel?"

"Nah. It was all bound to happen sooner or later. A lot of kids are glad he's gone. He's so whacked; they were afraid he'd turn North Creek into another Columbine."

"Listen, Joey," I said, changing the subject. "I also want to apologize for not returning your calls over the summer."

Joey sighed. "It's okay, Tee. I know you had your hands full. I just wanted you to know I was thinking about you and your old man. I considered stopping by your aunt's house a few times, but I wasn't sure if that might make things worse seeing how we broke up. How *is* Mel, Tee? My mom heard he's coming around."

"It's one day at a time," I replied, not really wanting to get into it.

"Any idea when he'll be coming home?"

I shook my head. "The doctors say he may be able to spend a few days at The Cabin over Christmas."

Joey grinned. "How is it, Tee, living with Jessica Fletcher?" It was no secret around town that Aunt George was first inspired to write mysteries while watching late night re-runs of "Murder, She Wrote."

"She's upbeat as usual. Keeps busy. But I know this situation with Mel is hard on her. She's got all this damn money, but none of it will buy Mel a new brain. All the doctors ever say is to 'give it time.'"

"How's your mom with all that's happened?" Joey asked.

I smirked. "You've probably heard what happened when she came up from Toronto while Mel was in intensive care; Moira Smith was on shift that night." Moira was an E.R. nurse and North Creek's biggest gossip, ten times worse than Rachel Lynde from the Anne of Green Gables stories. "I'm sure the tale of my hospital rampage made the full rounds before my tranquilizer wore off. But I'm on my way to see Lucy today. I want to try and patch things up."

"Good luck," Joey said.

"I'll need it. How's Vanessa?" I asked.

"We broke up Labour Day weekend."

I had to laugh. "Your city-girl wouldn't sleep with you either?"

"Why is that, do you suppose?" Joey looked genuinely baffled.

"You don't pace yourself, Joey," I grinned. "You move too fast. Remember those sex ed. seminars in Health class last spring? 'A good relationship should be like a cross-country marathon,' Coach Braden said. 'Not the hundred-metre dash.'"

Joey rolled his eyes. "Spoken like a distance runner. If I'd gone slower with you, would it have made a difference?"

I shrugged. "Maybe. I didn't say I'd never sleep with you, Joey. I just wasn't ready. I was still stretching and getting warmed up as you were sprinting towards the finish line. You need a girl like her," I said, opening the *Penthouse* and pointing to the sleazy centrefold.

"No argument here," Joey laughed, then asked, "What's going on with you and Newfie-Boy? I heard you were at his house last night."

"*What!*"

"So it's true," Joey smirked.

"Ethan and I were doing homework! How did you know I was there? All I need, Joey, to round out my miserable life, is a *stalker.*"

"Cool your jets, Tee," Joey said. "Bob Jacobs was in earlier this morning for smokes. He said he saw your Jeep out at the old Harper place when he passed on his way home last night; he lives just a few farms down."

"Ethan and I are just friends. Besides, he has a girlfriend back in Newfoundland," I explained.

"Not for long."

"What makes you an expert at long-distance love?" I sniped.

"Nothing," Joey replied. "But I was watching Ethan during English the other day; we both sit near the back. He looked at you three hundred and seventeen times in seventy minutes."

"You counted?"

"Beats listening to old Ms. Withers drone on about *The Stone Angel.*"

I was unconvinced. "So he looked at me. Big deal. I'm too busy for a boyfriend right now."

"So I guess you aren't interested in getting back together?"

"Not a chance."

A new customer pulled open the door and made a beeline for a display of windshield wiper fluid.

"I'm glad you stopped by today, Tee," Joey said.
"So am I."

I learned something about Mel that morning: he was a shameless flirt.

When I arrived, he was sitting at a table in the sunroom reading *Harry Potter and the Goblet of Fire* out loud to his speech therapist, a Julia Roberts look-a-like with "Deena, SLP" engraved on her name tag. Like he did when I was little, Mel was making up different voices for each character.

Deena, who'd been with Mel since the beginning of his therapy, since he could barely grunt his name or gesture for a glass of water, was grinning ear to ear.

"Hi," I said. "I'm sorry to interrupt story hour."

"Tee!" Mel exclaimed.

"I brought cookies for you, Dad." I gave Mel a kiss on the cheek.

"Is this another of your girlfriends, Mel?" Deena asked, winking at me. She knew who I was. The question was, did Mel?

"You are a girl and you are my friend," Mel grinned at Deena like a love-sick fool.

I smiled and said to Deena, "Better watch out for old Casanova here. Sounds like he's ready to ask you to marry him."

Mel turned to me, confused. "I'm already married."

Deena raised a brow. "To who?" she asked, feigning jealousy.

"Lucy. I Love Lucy. Mother Tree-sa," Mel said, looking solemn.

"Mother Teresa?" Deena gave me a shrug like maybe

Mel's delusions meant his recovery wasn't progressing as quickly as she'd first thought.

I found my voice. "He's right, mostly," I replied. "He used to be married to Lucy. And Lucy isn't Mother Teresa, but she is Theresa's mother. Get it? I'm Theresa."

Mel sat staring at his box of cookies.

"So, Dad?" I said, trying to refocus his attention. No response; "Dad" confused him sometimes. "Mel?" He looked up. "You and Lucy are divorced now. Not married anymore." I waited for him to ask why but he didn't. "You can marry Deena if you want to. If she'll have you," I grinned at Deena. "I don't object."

But Mel had left the building. Vacated. Gone to Carolina in his mind.

"Would you like a cookie?" I asked Deena, pointing to the box. She helped herself.

"They're delicious," she said a few seconds later, brushing oatmeal crumbs from her fingers. "Theresa baked them special for you, Mel. Try one."

"Okay." Mel shoved a cookie in his mouth. "Mmm," he mumbled and reached for another.

Deena motioned for me to join her in the hall.

"He's really in and out of it today," I remarked.

"Your father's memories are coming back faster now, but they're confusing him because the chronology is off. The next few weeks might be difficult for him. You have to expect some moodiness, maybe a tantrum."

"Will he ever be able to make sense of his memories?"

"Give it time."

I lost it. "All you doctors and therapists should have 'GIVE IT TIME' tattooed across your foreheads or embroidered on your lab coats!"

Deena nodded and sighed, "I know it's not a very good

answer. If I could wave a wand like Harry Potter and bring Mel back to normal for you, I would."

I felt like a heel. "I know. I'm sorry. I was rude."

"It's okay, Tee. You're human. You should be worried about boys and your nails and homework, not whether your father will have permanent amnesia and learn to cut his own meat again."

I waited, suspecting Deena had more to say.

"Listen, there's a group that meets Tuesday nights here at the Centre," she said. "It's for young people, teens like you, who have a parent or sibling receiving treatment. Maybe you could—"

I interrupted. "What is it? Group counselling? I'm really too busy for—"

"It's not counselling. The group is facilitated by a youth worker, but it's mostly a social program, a chance for kids who visit the Centre frequently to get to know each other and talk about—"

"And talk about our problems? No thanks. I've got enough—"

"Tee, hear me out," Deena said. "The kids do all sorts of things. Play basketball, cards, board games. Watch videos. Yeah, sometimes people talk about their problems and their fears, but mostly it's just an opportunity to connect with kids who understand what each other is going through."

"I'll think about it," I lied. "It's pretty far to drive on a school night. When I'm here, I'd rather spend my time with Mel."

"I understand," Deena said, though I doubted it. "Let me know if you change your mind." She waved goodbye to Mel and headed down the hall to see her next patient.

I wouldn't change my mind, of that I was sure. I supposed there were kids who got off being with others in the same boat, but not me. I feared I'd be jealous of kids whose parents only had two broken legs or a back brace and sorry for those whose parents were missing multiple limbs, who were quadriplegic, who'd need respirators for the rest of their lives. I didn't want to be in the same boat; I wanted to be in a different boat. I wanted to be in that cedar-strip canoe with Mel, paddling along the Rideau River.

I took Mel out for a short ride in his wheelchair before lunch. It was sunny and cool outside. Mel had spent the summer in a hospital bed; I hoped the fresh air would give his cheeks some colour.

Parked under a maple on the far side of the Centre grounds, I helped Mel with his arm exercises and told him I'd be leaving after lunch, travelling to Toronto to visit Lucy.

"By airplane?" he asked, gazing at a 747 passing overhead.

"No, I'm driving your Jeep," I said and held my breath.

If Mel was in his right mind, he'd have flipped. The old Mel worried like a demon when I was out in the Jeep alone, even if I was just driving to the local 7-Eleven for some milk. It wasn't *my* driving that worried him, he insisted, it was "the other guy." Maybe Mel realized now that just being a pedestrian could be as treacherous. Regardless, my immediate driving plans barely registered with him. Instead, he shouted, "Look, a turkey!" and pointed at a large black and white bird strutting across the parking lot.

"That's a Canada Goose, Dad. Getting ready to fly to his home in the south for the winter."

"I want to go home, too, Tee," Mel said slowly.

"You don't like it here, Dad?" I asked.

"I like my house better. I miss Lucy and Tree-sa-Jean."

"I'm Theresa-Jean," I said.

Mel shook his head. "Tree-sa-Jean is just a little girl. You are a big teenager."

Oh, God. Mel thought he was still married to Lucy and that Theresa-Jean was still a child.

It's progress, the doctors would say. Give it time.

I glanced at my watch. "Better get you in for lunch," I said to Mel.

Mel shook his head as we entered the cafeteria and patted what was left of his once rotund belly. "Not hungry. Ate too many cookies."

"Well, you can have some juice," I said, kissing him and passing him off to a lunchroom worker who parked him in front of a plate of tuna casserole and tied a huge plastic bib around his neck.

I pulled the car keys from my pants pocket; they were still attached to the little frog key chain I'd given to Mel for his birthday when I was six or seven. Mel stared at the keys and then twisted uncomfortably in his chair until he was gazing out the cafeteria window at the parking lot.

"Mel, you okay?" I asked.

"Watch out for the other guy."

# Chapter 7

I arrived in Toronto a little after four o'clock and made good time to Lucy's condo just north of Yonge and Finch.

"You look nice, Theresa," Lucy said. "That sweater's a good colour on you."

"You look good, too, Mom." But then, Lucy always looked good what with her buff fitness-instructor body and classy wardrobe.

"What's the plan?" I asked, piling my few packed belongings into the dresser in the spare room. I wasn't at Lucy's often enough to call the room mine, though more than once Lucy had offered to take me shopping for paint, curtains, and a comforter that would make me feel more at home.

Lucy stood in the doorway. "I thought maybe you'd like to go to the gym with me for an hour or so. Rachel asked if I'd cover her five-thirty Step class. I'll tell her no if you're tired or would rather eat now. The Red Lobster's not far from here."

I shook my head. "I'd love to work out for a while." My butt was numb from the long drive and I thought the exercise might calm my jitters. "We can dive head-first into the lobster linguine afterwards."

"Sounds fabulous," Lucy nodded.

"Let me drive?" I asked on our way to the parking garage. My mother had never experienced my driving; she left town before I got my licence.

"Okay," she said, her voice wary. "Theresa, did you mention to Mel you'd be driving his Jeep this weekend? That you'd be out cruising standard on the mean streets of Toronto?"

I nodded and grinned. "He didn't try to stop me."

Lucy laughed then, a deep, confident laugh I had never heard before. "You better hope he doesn't get his wits back this weekend."

*"Basic right for three, two, one, hop-turn, v-step left for three, two, one, hop-turn, four jacks, turn-step left, over the top for four ..."*

You had to hand it to Lucy; she was great at her job. Her Step patterns were fast-paced and challenging, her music was loud and energetic, and she had enthusiasm that just wouldn't quit. The participants in her class really pushed themselves and sweat buckets. Lucy seemed so sure of herself, not at all like the mother I knew who cried every time I looked at her sideways. She really came alive. I dare say I was proud of her.

We lathered up side by side in the group shower; the private stalls had all been taken by the time I helped Lucy stack the risers and lock up the sound equipment. I'd spent enough time in school and hockey locker rooms not to be self-conscious about my body.

"You've lost weight, Theresa," Lucy said as we dried off.

I shrugged. "Maybe a few pounds"

"Are you eating okay?"

"Yeah."

"Working out more?"

I shook my head. "I still run every other day, but nothing extra. Volleyball hasn't started yet."

"Hmm," Lucy pondered, but I knew it was stress that had put my metabolism into overdrive.

"I'll be okay, Mom," I said. "I needed to lose a few pounds anyway." Being Joey's girlfriend had meant a lot of burger dates, pizza-and-video dates, movie-and-buttered-popcorn dates; I'd consumed more calories last winter than even running could chase away.

"Well, you don't need to lose any more. I'll send you back with a case of energy bars from the cafeteria upstairs. I get a discount."

"Thanks," I said, hunting through our locker for my underwear. I wondered if it bothered Lucy that for the first time in years, my stomach was flatter than hers.

"You're lucky you have your Aunt Georgina's breasts," Lucy remarked good-humouredly as I fastened my bra. If breasts were citrus fruit, mine were grapefruit and Lucy's were clementines. To be honest, I wished mine were smaller; they were a pain, sometimes literally, during long runs.

"And your father's height," Lucy continued. "And brains. Regardless of what he's like now, it's *his* smarts you inherited."

"What do I have of yours?" I asked, assuming she'd be stumped.

Lucy answered right away. "My energy."

"Guess I turned out okay," I replied.

"Theresa, you're fabulous."

It was like my mother had been hit in the head, too.

After dinner at Red Lobster, Lucy and I stayed up watching a four-hour TV broadcast of *Gone with the Wind*; Lucy was an old movie buff. With our bare feet on her coffee table and a bowl of microwave popcorn between us, we sat engrossed in the stormy Confederate lives of Scarlett O'Hara and Rhett Butler until the final credits rolled at one a.m.

"That was fun," I said as Lucy rinsed the popcorn bowl and I tossed our Diet Coke cans into the recycling box under her sink.

"Sure was," Lucy said, patting my arm. "Sleep well."

I lay in bed listening to the late night traffic on Yonge Street and thinking about my mother in the other room. Neither of us had mentioned what happened between us last summer. Once again, it seemed we'd agreed by silent consensus to let the storm pass. But my episode at the hospital had blown in like a Level Five tornado; there needed to be some serious rebuilding. I hoped Lucy and I were breaking ground this weekend. Our previous relationship had the substance of a nylon tent: a thin foundation, shaky poles, and little to shelter us from the wind and rain except Mel, whom I shamelessly used as a buffer while Lucy got left out in the cold. How many times had she tried to interest me in one of her old movies back in North Creek? Dozens. Had I ever sat through one? Never. I'd really enjoyed the movie tonight and our time together. Maybe Scarlett O'Hara had it right; tomorrow was another day.

The next morning we took the subway to Harbourfront and caught the ten-fifteen ferry to Ward's Island. It was a brilliant morning, but cool, and the crowds were sparse.

Our day was idyllic. The last time I'd been to the

Toronto Islands was as a small child when Lucy and Mel had brought me to the city for a week-long summer getaway. We'd visited the Zoo, the Royal Ontario Museum, the Islands, and the Ontario Science Centre. It was one of my few memories of Mel, Lucy and I having fun together as a threesome, a family.

"Aren't those cottages charming?" Lucy asked now as we toured the narrow lanes of tiny homes.

"Do people really live here year-round?" I asked.

"Sure," Lucy replied. "There's a school, a fire hall, a community centre. Many residents are writers and artists inspired by the peaceful atmosphere. Others commute by ferry each day to jobs downtown. It's the best of both worlds."

I remembered something. "When we came to the Islands before, we went to the amusement park. Centreville. There was an antique carousel with all different animals. You took a photograph. Mel was riding a bear and I was beside him on the ostrich."

Lucy smiled. "You have a good memory."

*Too good*, I thought. I also remembered the horrible fight Mel and Lucy had on the way home from our until-then perfect Toronto vacation. Just before we left for home, Mel surprised me with the large chemistry set I'd ogled at the Science Centre gift shop. Lucy thought the age recommendation 12+ was too advanced for a seven-year-old, even a bright one. She was afraid I'd blow up the house. Mel yelled at Lucy. I yelled at Lucy. Lucy cried for awhile. Then we drove all the way home in silence. I don't know what became of the chemistry set; whatever magic it held for me had been lost that afternoon. Chemistry was still my worst subject.

I shook the bad memories away and walked with Lucy along the Ward's Island boardwalk. We rented bicycles at the foot of the pier and spent an hour touring Hanlan's Point. Lucy pointed out the airport, the "haunted" lighthouse, and the trail that led to the "clothing-optional" beach. Later, we sat near the fountains, ate jumbo hotdogs, and watched seagulls patrol the Lake Ontario shore.

Then Lucy dropped the bomb.

"There's someone I'd like you to meet tomorrow," she said. We'd arrived home from the Islands at five and were in Lucy's kitchen making salad for dinner.

"A man?" I raised a brow. I debated telling Lucy that Mel thought they were still married, but decided against it. Who knew how long his delusion would last, and it wasn't like I harboured any secret desires to get them back together.

Lucy shrugged. "Yes, a man. He's a doctor. I've been seeing him once or twice a week for a couple months now."

"Okay," I said. I didn't want to meet her boyfriend, doctor or not, but I was determined not to get into a scuffle over anything this weekend. I didn't want to blow it just when it looked like Lucy and I might get through a whole weekend without one of us resorting to screams, sarcasm, or tears.

If she wants me to meet him, it must be serious, I thought. I cringed at the thought of having to deal with a potential new stepfather on top of everything else.

"I know it's probably not something you're too comfortable about, but—" Lucy started.

"It's okay, Mom. I'll meet the doctor."

Lucy shot me a weird look, perhaps wondering if my body had been possessed by the spirit of a cooperative child. "Thanks for understanding, Theresa," she said.

It would be a while before she'd say that again.

"We're meeting in his *office*?" I asked the next afternoon. Lucy and I had slept in and grabbed a quick lunch at Cultures before driving in separate cars to a small stone house off Bayview. I would be leaving after the "meeting" to head back to North Creek. I'd called Aunt George to say I'd be home for dinner.

The house had immaculate gardens and a silver BMW in the driveway. I parked the Jeep on the street and followed Lucy around the side to a door marked "OFFICE: Dr. Mark Spellman."

"Where else would we be meeting him?" Lucy looked confused.

I raised a brow, but remained silent. A coffee shop? The mall? His living room?

Lucy rang the bell. When the door opened, I gasped. I couldn't help myself.

"Hello, Lucy," a man said, gazing up at me and extending his hand. "You must be Theresa."

"Hi." I gave his hand a limp shake, all the while thinking my mother had truly lost it. Dr. Spellman was *ancient*, at least sixty, and bald except for the coarse grey hair that sprouted from his ears. And he was short. My mother is barely five-two; Dr. Spellman, in shoes, came up to her nose.

"Please come in." Dr. Spellman led us through a small foyer into what looked like a waiting room. There were several leather couches, peaceful landscapes on the walls, and a few tables displaying magazines and pamphlets titled: "Surviving a Sibling's Suicide"; "Depression, Divorce, and You"; "When Schizophrenia Hits Home."

"Please have a seat," he gestured. He then offered us coffee, which we declined.

I kept trying to catch Lucy's eye so I could officially register my confusion, but as if she could sense my discomfort, she avoided glancing my way.

I've never been shy. I got that from Mel, who always said the only fools in the world were those who never asked questions. I'd been a fool the previous night for not asking Lucy more about this Dr. Spellman character. Was she *in love* with him? Why did she call him Dr. Spellman and not Mark? Did he need a booster seat when they went to dinner or the movies?

"So, what kind of doctor are you?" I asked. Judging by the huge box of toys in one corner and the shelf of picture books and puppets, I guessed pediatrician; he was, after all, the same height as a fourth-grader. But where was his examining room?

Dr. Spellman flashed his dentures. "I'm not a medical doctor, Theresa. I'm a psychologist, a family therapist." He smiled benignly. "Your mother didn't tell you?"

I shook my head, raised a brow at Lucy, and laughed out loud. "Kind of ironic isn't it, you dating a family therapist?"

"Dating?" Lucy's eyes grew wide with genuine horror. *"Dating?"* she repeated.

"You said you wanted me to meet a man you've been seeing, that he was a doctor—Oh my God!" I shouted, as reality sunk its teeth into my jugular. "He's not your *boyfriend*; he's your *shrink*!"

"I'm a family therapist," Dr. Spellman corrected. "I mentioned to your mother at our last session that it would be helpful for me to meet you."

"It might have been helpful to *me* if she hadn't *tricked* me into coming here today. You're wasting your time." I stood up and glared at Lucy.

"Theresa, please, sit down." She put a hand on my arm. "I'm sorry," she turned to Dr. Spellman. "It seems there's been a misunderstanding."

I shrugged off Lucy's hand and ignored her pleas to calm down. "You think I'm *crazy*? Is that it?" I yelled.

"Nobody's *crazy*, Theresa," Lucy pleaded. "I was hoping if I got some help and you met Dr. Spellman, we could get along better, that I could be a better mother to you."

"You waited seventeen years, Lucy! What's the rush?" I raged. "Or do you feel sorry for me because Mel currently has the mental capacity of a garden salad? We were doing fine until *this*." I pointed to Dr. Spellman, who sat calmly observing my tirade. I turned my anger on him. "Everything bad she's told you about me is true! I'm a terrible, *crazy* daughter!" Then I turned back to Lucy. "You're pulling extra shifts at the Y to pay for *this*? Give it up, Lucy. Give *me* up!" I yanked open the door to the foyer.

"Please, Theresa!" Lucy was standing now too. "I don't want you to go away angry."

I glared at her for a long moment, then—in a dark voice I barely recognized as my own—said, "Frankly, my dear, I don't give a damn."

Lucy arrived at Aunt George's before I did; in my blind fury, I'd missed the 401 on-ramp and made several circles around the city before finding it again. Then, of course, I'd needed to gas up.

Lucy was hunched over on the porch glider. She looked like hell, her face red and puffy from crying. Aunt George was perched beside her, a strong hand on Lucy's shoulder.

Without a word to either, I bounded up the porch steps, yanked open the screen door and let it slam behind me.

I ran to my room and slammed that door, too. The clock

over my desk read five-forty-six p.m. How could things have gone from hopeful to hell in less than five hours?

It wasn't until the focus of my anger shifted from my mother to myself that I started to bawl. I'd wanted things to work between me and Lucy. I'd made an effort. Had this current mess really been just a stupid misunderstanding on my part? And what bothered me more? That Lucy was in counselling, or my own guilt for making her feel she needed it?

At seven, there was a rap at my door. I ignored it. Aunt George waited a few minutes, then barged in and plunked into an armchair near the bed where I lay on my back staring at the ceiling and dreaming up ways to break both legs so I could go live at the Centre with Mel. Harley padded in behind Aunt George, stretched herself out on the bed beside me, and rested her heavy head on my lap.

"Getting hungry?" Aunt George asked.

I shook my head, said nothing.

A few long minutes passed. Finally, Aunt George cleared her throat. "Theresa, I'm not clear about what happened with you and Lucy today, but if you're upset about her bringing you to see Dr. Spellman, blame me. I spoke to her last week and told her I agreed with the doctor, that it would be a good idea for him to meet you. And for you to meet him."

"*Why?*" I croaked. "Things were going so well this weekend. We went to the gym and watched *Gone with the Wind* and toured the Islands…"

Aunt George nodded. "I know. Lucy told me. It's a good start, but you aren't playmates, Theresa; you're mother and daughter and you need each other, especially now. And you're too old to be having public temper tantrums every time Lucy makes a decision you don't agree with, to be running from her at the first sign of trouble. You don't have Mel to run to anymore."

*"What?"* I sat up. I'd always blamed myself for the problems between Mel and Lucy, but did Aunt George blame me, too? I thought she was my ally.

"Theresa, Mel is my little brother and I love him dearly, but he didn't make it easy for you and Lucy to get along when you were growing up."

"Lucy and I have nothing in common," I said, defensive on Mel's behalf.

Aunt George shook her head. "Even if that were true, and I'm not sure it is, it's no excuse to shut someone out of your life."

"Lucy and I never saw eye to eye."

"Mel spoiled you rotten."

"He loved me!"

Aunt George was losing her patience. "He did and he does and he will again, but you shouldn't confuse his love with his indulgence. Your mother loves you, too—just as much—by trying to set limits with you. Theresa, by the time you were three years old, you'd learned that whatever you wanted, an extra cookie, a new toy, sympathy when Lucy scolded you, all you had to do was run to Mel."

So it was common knowledge: I had Mel eating out of my hands; Lucy was the one who made me wash them before dinner.

Aunt George continued. "You're old enough to understand that when there are two parents raising a kid, it should be a team effort. But from day one Mel appointed himself leader, chief parent. Lucy finally gave up."

"On me?"

"No, Theresa. On herself. With Mel, you were all sweetness and light, Little Miss Maturity, Mel's prodigy. With Lucy, you were, and still *are* I might add, a tyrant."

"So everything is my fault?" I knew it. I just *knew* it.

"It's not your fault!" Aunt George shouted. "Yes, you took advantage of the situation, but you didn't *create* the situation. That was Lucy and Mel's doing." She reached out and ran her hand through my hair. "Lucy's leaving at nine, Theresa. She needs to work in the morning."

"She didn't have to drive all the way here today."

"Yes, she did. She was worried sick what with you being so angry and a fairly new driver on a busy highway. She's terrified of losing you, Theresa. Lucy may have given up trying to raise you, but she never stopped loving you. Take my word for it. You're all she has now."

"She should have considered that when she slept with creepy Harold."

"Don't be too hard on her."

"How can you say that after what she did to Mel?"

"I don't agree with all her choices, Theresa, but Lucy is my friend. The marriage was doomed long before Harold."

"I guess." I blew my nose. Lucy and Mel had been fighting as long as I could remember, usually about me. Harold gave my parents a tangible reason to divorce. It had been easiest to blame Lucy for their breakup and stop blaming myself. Now I knew better.

Aunt George kissed my hair, scratched Harley behind the ears, and announced she was going to take a bath. She'd be downstairs by nine, she said, to say goodbye to Lucy. She walked towards the door.

"What should I do?" I asked.

Aunt George turned back. "Do what's in your heart."

I knew going to Lucy, offering up the olive branch, was the only way to budge the boulder of sorrow pressing down on my chest. Aunt George had given me a lot to think about, but the idea that kept crowding me was that Lucy still loved me. Interesting hypothesis, but how to test?

When I padded into the kitchen, Lucy was hunched at the oak table, her face etched with exhaustion. She set her mug of tea down as I approached. Before she could make the first move, I leaned down, wrapped my arms around her, and whispered, "I'm so sorry, Mom," in her ear. Lucy turned in her seat, buried her head in my shoulder, and held onto me for dear life.

It had been more than ten years since I'd let my mother hug me, at least five since she'd stopped trying. Even though I was bigger than Lucy now, there was something about her embrace, maybe her smell or touch, that made me feel tiny but powerful, something that proved to me I was still Lucy's daughter and indisputably loved.

# Part 2

*The care of rivers is not a question of rivers, but of the human heart.*

– Tanako Shozo

# Chapter 8

As autumn progressed and the outdoor world prepared for hibernation, my own world was budding.

"Giving it time" was in fact bringing Mel back. He still had serious amnesia, but the algebra hadn't been a fluke—he could really do it. His speech was still slurred and painfully slow, but he'd begun reading adult fiction again. Mel progressed from the walker to a cane and could make it to the bathroom and back unassisted. He'd started requesting things like Chinese food and spinach lasagna on take-out nights.

I called Lucy every few days. To suggest our relationship had become the stuff of Hallmark cards would be a gross exaggeration, but we were trying to bridge the gorge between merely talking at each other and communicating. I reluctantly agreed to go with Lucy to see Dr. Spellman the next time I visited Toronto on the condition he wouldn't make me lie on the couch or ask about my sex life.

"What sex life?" Lucy asked, amused. She knew now about my breakup with Joey, the sex maniac-in-training. She told me, in a more matter-of-fact manner than I thought possible, that if I met a guy I did want to sleep with not to hesitate coming to her for advice.

"I already know not to do it on the kitchen floor if Mel's on his way home," I said. I couldn't help myself.

"I guess I deserved that," Lucy said after a few long, silent seconds.

I tried for a save. "Sorry. I know what you meant. Birth control and stuff, right?"

"Right."

"And back to Dr. Spellman, I just don't think my sex life or lack thereof is his business one way or the other."

"I agree," Lucy said. "And just in case you're wondering, Theresa, I don't have a sex life right now, either. You don't have to worry about me introducing you to any wannabe stepfathers anytime soon."

"Thank God for that. Did Aunt George tell you Mel thinks he's still married to you?"

Lucy laughed, not at all bothered by Mel's confusion. "She says he asks about me almost every day. That he specifically asked that I come to his Thanksgiving dinner party at the Centre."

"Maybe when Mel sees you this time, he'll remember."

"Then I hope I get to finish my pumpkin pie before he tosses me out the door."

"Why did you agree to come?" I asked. I couldn't believe spending a major holiday with a mentally challenged ex-spouse was anyone's idea of fun.

"I love him, Theresa." Even over the phone her tone told me she meant it, really and truly meant it.

It was on the tip of my tongue to ask Lucy why she cheated on Mel. My strong feelings for Ethan had made me wonder more than once if I was in fact my mother's daughter. What was worse, to cheat on your own husband, or to mess around with a man you know is with someone else? If Ethan put the moves on me, would I be able to resist on the grounds that he had a girlfriend five provinces away, or would I seize the day? But instead I asked Lucy, "Why is it Dad remembers you and not Aunt George or me?"

"I don't know, Theresa," she said. But something in her tone suggested to me that maybe she did.

"I'll call again on the weekend," I said.

"I'd like that," Lucy replied. She seemed lonely to me lately. I wondered if she'd always been that way and I just hadn't noticed.

North Creek High's annual Thanksgiving Dance was, next to the Grad, *the* social occasion of the school year. Admission was ten dollars worth of non-perishables for the local food bank per person.

"Hey, Tee." Joey sauntered up to me after gym class a week before the big event. "You and Newfie-boy going to the dance together?"

I shook my head. "Ethan's going East to see his girl-friend next weekend."

Joey raised a brow. "You okay with that?"

I wasn't sure. I wanted to be, but Ethan and I spent a lot of time together. Besides our classes, we got together outside of school at least once a week to do homework, play chess, and take Ernie, Bert and Harley for runs by the river. I felt comfortable talking with him about anything; in fact, it was Ethan who urged me not to be too closed-minded about Dr. Spellman, who got me thinking maybe my mother and I *could* use a little mediation through the dark holes of our relationship.

Ethan confided he'd been sent for counselling when he was in fourth grade and suddenly began acting out in class.

Ellie had just been diagnosed with CF and he'd taken it upon himself to read up on it in the Stephenville library. Skimming over the description of the disease and treatment options, Ethan had zeroed in on the phrase *"prognosis is always fatal."* He'd been jealous when Ellie was a baby, he admitted; he'd thought having their own "flesh and blood" kid would mean his parents would love him, their "adopted" kid, less. Ethan concluded that his ambivalent feelings for his sister had caused her disease. The counsellor helped him sort out his feelings of guilt and jealousy and made him realize how good it would be for Ellie to have a big brother to play with and teach her things. The counsellor had also explained that CF, while life-threatening, could be managed.

Despite all the time we spent together, Ethan and I had never crossed the line between "just friends" and "more than friends." If Ethan could tell I was attracted to him, he never let on and never tried to distance himself from me. I never let on that, despite his supposed commitment to Tina, he seemed a little attracted to me, too. I worried if and how his Thanksgiving in Newfoundland would change that.

"Why should I care?" I asked Joey, hoping I sounded appropriately indifferent.

"Want to go with me, then?"

"With you? To the dance?"

Joey grinned. "For old time's sake." The Thanksgiving Dance was where he and I hooked up the previous year. A little smooth talk at the refreshment table, a few slow dances and I was smitten. Book-smart, sexually naïve Tee falls on her face for street-smart, jock-boy Joey—then gets dumped just in time for summer vacation.

"I don't want to get back together with you." I was surprised how easy this was for me to say. But then I'd never had time to entertain a broken heart with Joey. I'd needed it fully operational to deal with Mel.

"Then we can just go as friends. Ethan is your friend. Why can't I be your friend?"

"Ethan's never tried to rip my bra off with his teeth."

"It's only a matter of time. He's crazy for you. How much you want to bet he breaks it off with his Newfie girl-friend this weekend?"

"Okay. I'll go to the dance with you," I said, just to shut Joey up.

Friday, the day of the dance, I was at a table in the cafeteria playing poker for Mini-Ritz crackers with Ethan and two guys from his Physics class. The way I was creaming them, I was likely to have my lost pounds back by the end of the semester. I knew girls made snide comments about me being a tomboy and laughed when I chose to play cards with the "techno-geeks" instead of following them to the plaza to try on new lipstick colours. Except for Leona Brown, who'd moved to Saskatoon, and who, like me, was good at math and sports, I'd never had close girlfriends. It wasn't that I had any confusion about my sexuality; I just didn't need to talk about it all the time like some girls did. I'd been quizzed to death when I started seeing Joey. Did we do this? Did we do that? As far as I was concerned, what we did and didn't do was nobody's business. The girls were looking for dirt, but I wasn't serving. Besides, it had been standard PG fare, despite Joey's attempts for more.

When the bell rang for third period, Joey came up behind me, grabbed a handful of crackers from my pile and stuffed them in his mouth. "So," he said, spewing little pieces of Ritz at me. "I'll pick you up at seven?"

I shrugged. "I can meet you in town, at your place or at school. It doesn't make sense for you to drive all the way out to Birch Lane then have you turn right around and come back to North Creek."

"You're my *date*, Tee," Joey said. "I'll pick you up. It's the chivalrous thing to do, isn't it?"

Actually, I thought he was just looking for an excuse to borrow his dad's BMW, but why argue? "Anything you say, Prince Charming." If he caught the irony in my sentiment, he let it go.

Out of the corner of my eye, I watched Ethan wad up his lunch bag, wave to the guys, gather up his books and leave the table without so much as a glance in my direction.

"Ethan!" I called. We had Chemistry next and usually walked to class together.  He kept going.

"Why didn't you wait for me?" I asked, plunking down beside him on one of the wobbly green lab stools behind our workstation.

He shrugged. "I guess I didn't hear you."

"Bull. What's eating you?"

Dead silence for a count of ten. Finally, Ethan grew tired of me staring at him. "You're going to the dance with *Joey*?" he asked. "I thought you guys were past tense?"

Why do you care? I was dying to retort. Aren't you going to Newfoundland to get laid this weekend? Instead I shrugged. "We're just going as friends. In North Creek, it's not cool to show up for school dances without a date."

"I would've gone with you," Ethan said.

"But you're going to Newfoundland, aren't you?" I was baffled.

"I couldn't get a flight until tomorrow morning."

"I'm sorry, Ethan. Joey asked me and I couldn't think of

any reason to say no." I felt uncomfortable all of a sudden. Odd, until that point, Ethan and I had talked so openly about all sorts of personal and painful issues. We'd analyzed my relationship with my mother, with Mel, even with Aunt George. We'd discussed his relationship with Ellie, with his adoptive parents, with Tina. But we'd never discussed *our* relationship. It was like if we didn't talk about it, no one would get hurt. I hadn't accepted the date with Joey to make Ethan jealous. Had I?

"It's okay, Tee. I just was thinking…. Oh, never mind what I was thinking. Besides, I have a Physics assignment to get done tonight; I don't want to end up dragging my books East with me. I'll hit the college library tonight. It's open late."

I was going to ask Ethan if he wanted to meet me and Joey after the dance for a burger, but Mr. Harnett came by and told us to stop wasting our brain cells on idle chatter. Ethan and I spent the rest of the period trying to focus on our test tubes and lab notes, but we had to confess to Mr. Harnett at the end of class that the results of our experiments were inconclusive. He looked at our notes, then at each of us in turn.

"Don't make things more complicated than they have to be."

"You look great, Theresa!" Aunt George exclaimed later that evening.

I'd pulled off what Mel had once jokingly dubbed "The Transformation" in a little under a half-hour. After a quick dinner, I'd dashed to the shower, defuzzed, and then spent too long searching for my one and only non-sports bra, a little black thin-strapped underwire. I'd slipped on a simple black tank dress and surveyed the results. Not bad. My arms were still tan from my summer day camp job, and I was toned, a fact generally hidden under my baggy pants and sweatshirts. The weight loss wasn't so pronounced that I'd lost my curves. Joey, eat your heart out, I thought, and made myself laugh. With ten minutes left to spare, I smoothed my hair with leave-in conditioner, put in gold hoop earrings, and did my eyes in wild autumn colours. My nails were a mess, bitten down and ragged, so I left them alone—no point drawing attention to them with polish. I fell short of gorgeous by a large margin, but for a girl who never read *Cosmo* and avoided the mall like a tropical virus, I didn't shine up too badly.

"Too bad your friend Ethan's not going to the dance," Aunt George said, not bothering to disguise the amusement in her voice. She'd met him a few weeks back when he'd come over to work on an English presentation. "I thought you hated group projects?" she'd teased me afterwards. She hadn't made a big deal out of me going to the dance with Joey—I could have told her Godzilla was coming to pick me up; she was just happy I was taking a break from school and Mel for a night and showing an interest in something she saw as a normal teenage thing.

"Is everything ready for Mel's dinner party tomorrow?" I asked, pointedly ignoring the comment about Ethan.

Aunt George nodded. "We're all set. The room's booked at the Centre. Food is ready to go. Lucy'll be here by ten tomorrow morning so we can all arrive together."

"You sure this party is a good idea?"

"He's looking forward to it; you know Thanksgiving is Mel's favourite holiday. He was beside himself with excitement when I told him Lucy was coming."

"But he remembers the Lucy he loved, not the one he

divorced. What if her being there upsets him?"

"He still loves her, Theresa."

"He *thinks* he still loves her."

"No. He *still* loves her. He's loved her since they met at McGill."

"How can you love someone and just let them go? Mel's the one who told Lucy to leave. She wanted to stay, try to work things out. They thought the bungalow walls were soundproof, but I heard a lot."

"You've never been in love, have you, Theresa?" Aunt George asked.

I heard crunching gravel in the drive followed by the familiar beep of the BMW's horn. Classy jerk wouldn't even come to the door. No, Aunt George, I thought, I've never been in love.

"Gotta go." I gave Aunt George a quick hug and a kiss on the cheek. "I'll be home by midnight."

I should have known; St. Mary's girls were at the dance.

St. Mary's was a private Catholic girls' school on the outskirts of town. Since there were no private boys' schools in the region, the St. Mary's girls were often invited to North Creek's social functions. Tonight there were at least ten of them gathered around the refreshment table looking shockingly slutty in blood-red lipstick and dresses so short that their butt cheeks showed when they bent even slightly. If they felt uncomfortable as singles sharing a gymnasium with a hundred North Creek couples, they didn't show it. Rather, they seemed up to the challenge of moving right in.

And it wasn't like Joey minded. After a few dances with me, he invited a few of the St. Mary's girls to sit at our table and proceeded to give them his ogle-eyed attention.

I pushed my chair back. "I'm going to mingle," I said, leaving Joey to entertain his Catholic harem. I don't think he even heard me, so taken was he with a red-headed, pouty-lipped girl who put her hand on his knee every time he made her laugh, which was often. Joey was many things, in hindsight mostly negative, but he did know how to make a first impression. A few minutes later, from across the room, I watched him disappear with Miss Pouty Lips out the side door that led to the parking lot. Damn, I knew I should have brought the Jeep into town.

I ran into a couple of guys from Geography who'd risked the life-long "dork" label by showing up stag. I danced with both of them. I talked awhile to one of the teacher chaperones about her summer vacation spent volunteering at an orphanage in Kenya. I nursed a Diet Coke and wished Ethan was there. Get over it, Tee, I chastised myself. He's going to Newfoundland this week-end to be with his girlfriend. The one he keeps in his heart.

"There you are!" Joey materialized beside me just as a slow dance was announced. He wasn't a great dancer, but he was too sure of himself to care. I expected his confident touch to bring back a tingle of feeling left over from last spring, but I felt nothing. I was almost disappointed. I didn't want Joey back, but I missed the feeling of being close to someone. My hormones had gone into hibernation that summer; Mel had been the one and only man in my life. But with Mel slowly emerging from the woods, my sexuality had reawakened with a vengeance. My hormones were primed and ready for action. But was I?

Joey kissed my neck. I pulled back.

"Have you been smoking weed?" My question was largely rhetorical. "Eau du Cannabis" overpowered Joey's usual Old Spice.

"One of the St. Mary's girls gave me a drag off a joint in the parking lot."

"Just a drag?" I'd seen Joey smoke pot at house parties a few times and "just a drag" never made him shifty-eyed or giggly the way he was now.

"What is this, Tee?" he asked. "You never minded before that I smoked."

"That was before."

"Tee, don't let this thing with your father get to you. I haven't been drinking, and I won't be. And I'll be totally straight to get you home later. Maybe you should come out and take a few drags, too; you seem tense."

"I don't think so, Joey."

Joey laughed and let me go. "Don't be a party-pooper, Tee. A few of the St. Mary's girls are bored. They're going to grab a burger over at Harvey's. Want to join them?" He looked hopeful.

"You go ahead," I said, knowing it was what he wanted to hear. "And don't worry about taking me home. I'll get a ride with Frank and Lisa; they're out my way."

"You sure?" Joey asked, looking relieved. "I don't want you to think I'm running out on you."

"Wouldn't be the first time," I snapped. "Just go. And don't ask me out again. Ever. I'd rather stay home and floss."

"What's up? Are you on the rag or something? It was *you* that wanted to come as 'just friends.' Don't blame me if the St. Mary's chicks are interested in knowing me other ways." He ran off to catch up with Miss Pouty Lips.

"Have a nice Thanksgiving, you big turkey," I muttered.

It was only ten-thirty, and Frank and Lisa were lip-locked in a dark corner. I didn't want to ask for a ride home when it seemed pretty clear they'd be heading somewhere to park after the dance.

I knew Aunt George would come in a flash, but she was writing tonight and I didn't want to interrupt. She had so little time for herself these days.

I danced a few more times with the Geography boys to kill time, then grabbed another pop and went out into the deserted hall for some air. If I waited until the dance was over, I could catch a ride home with Mrs. Dorset, who was running the sound system; she lived along River Road, too.

"Excuse me?" I heard a familiar voice behind me. "I'm looking for a young woman named Tee. She's your height, same nose and chin, but she wears denim and flannel and cotton, not—God, Tee, you look…. Wow!" Ethan grinned.

Joey hadn't said a word about "The Transformation." True, he'd seen me dressed up before, but still, it wouldn't have killed him to…. Oh, who cares, I reminded myself. He and I were ancient history.

"*Ethan?*"

"I finished at the library and was across at Harvey's grabbing a late dinner. Joey was there with a female entourage."

"St. Mary's girls."

"Not nuns-in-training, that's for sure. He looked stoned."

"He was."

"Are you okay? I know Joey used to be your boyfriend—"

"Joey's not much of a friend, boy or otherwise," I interrupted. "I was an idiot to agree to this."

"Need a ride home?" Ethan asked.

I nodded. "I'd really appreciate that. But Ethan?" I couldn't help laughing.

"Hmm?"

"You have to stop staring at my boobs."

Ethan raised his eyes, then laughed. "Sorry," he said, not sounding sorry at all.

Some kid came out into the hall and yelled "Last dance!"

"Want to dance?" I asked Ethan.

"I'm not dressed for a dance. I haven't paid, or—"

"I doubt you'll get jail time."

Ethan took my hand. "Then, sure. I'd love to."

In the dark of the gym, no one took notice of Ethan's Levi's and polar fleece jacket. The last song started to play; it was "Feels Like Home," by Chantal Kreviazuk.

His hands found my waist. I rested mine on his glorious biceps, hoping he couldn't tell my legs were weak. I wondered if he felt the electricity that was shooting from my fingertips into the soft fleece of his jacket.

Towards the end of the song, Ethan pulled me closer and let his hands wander a little, nothing suggestive, just enough to let me know this was more than an obligatory dance for him, too. This can't be happening, I thought. Ethan will be in Newfoundland, taking Tina in his arms, in less than fourteen hours.

When the music ended, Ethan held me for a few extra seconds until the gym lights came on. "Happy Thanksgiving, everyone!" Mrs. Dorset shouted over the sounds of scraping chairs and pop cans being hurled into recycling bins.

When Ethan turned the pickup into Aunt George's driveway a little after eleven-thirty, the evening rain had ended and the stars were out in all their glory.

He walked me to the door, past the wary eyes of the grizzly and moose.

"Want to come in for some hot chocolate?" I asked. Not the sexiest pick-up line, I knew.

Ethan shook his head. "I better get going. I have that early plane to catch."

I nodded. "Make it back safely," I said. My big selfish fear right then was that he'd get back to Newfoundland and decide to stay after all.

Ethan smiled, making no move to leave. Instead he took a step towards me, gazed into my eyes, and shifted his head like he was gearing up to kiss me. I knew if he did, I'd kiss back, even though I knew it was wrong, something my mother would do.

As if reading my mind, Ethan straightened up suddenly and took a step back, banging his shoulder on the grizzly. "Have a great time at your father's party tomorrow," he croaked. "Happy Thanksgiving." And then he was gone.

# Chapter 9

Mel's Thanksgiving party was, in three words, very, *very* weird.

Lucy, Aunt George and I arrived at the Centre a little after noon in Aunt George's Ford Expedition. The official plan was for Lucy and me to get dinner going in the reserved party room while Aunt George would go up to Mel's room to make sure he was shaved and had his shirt on right-side-out. The therapists were making him do most things for himself now, and the results were sometimes, let's say, not up to dinner-party standards.

Lucy looked stunning as usual in a green wool dress. Her hair had been cut in a short perky style that suited her fine features. I looked like a lanky Spruce tree standing next to her in bark-brown dress pants and a forest-green sweater.

"How was the dance last night?" Lucy asked. I'd mentioned the dance to her a few days ago when I called to tell her about my third place finish in the regional 10k cross-country finals. I told her Joey and I were going as friends, but that I wasn't interested in getting back together with him.

"It was okay," I shrugged. I wasn't in the best of spirits, having tossed and turned the whole night being alternately mad at Joey, confused with Ethan, and anxious about tonight's party with Mel.

"Plenty of fish in the sea," Lucy replied. She knew as well as I that the sea was a long way from North Creek. Besides, the only fish I was interested in hooking, the Atlantic Ethan, was caught in someone else's net.

Mel shuffled in awhile later looking sharp in crisp khakis and the thick navy sweater I'd given him last Christmas. He engulfed me in a bear hug. His eyes were bright; he seemed alert and in good spirits.

I hugged him back, kissed his cheek, and told him he looked great.

"Hey kid," Mel grinned. "Guess what—"

"Hold that thought, Dad," I interrupted as I heard the potatoes boil over. Quite frankly, I wasn't in the mood to hear another one of Mel's nonsensical riddles.

"I'll get it," Lucy said quickly.

"No, it's okay. I got it," I said to her.

"But—"

I waved her off. "Go say hi to Mel."

I turned down the heat on the potatoes, keeping an eye trained on my parents. Civility between them was all I really hoped for.

But I got so much more. More than I bargained for.

"Lucy!" Mel laughed. "God, I've missed you so much!" He tossed his cane to the floor and wrapped his arms around her, holding on like she was a life raft and he was lost at sea. Then Mel kissed Lucy. It wasn't a friendly peck, or even a smooch. It was a soul kiss, the kiss of two lovers separated by time and distance coming together once again. Joey and I had done our fair share of kissing during our relationship, but nothing came within a mile of what I was witnessing. Come to think of it, nothing I'd seen on TV or at the movies came close either; Mel and Lucy weren't acting. What the hell was going on?

Aunt George motioned me out of the room and shut the door behind us. "Let's give them some privacy."

I started to pace the hall. "I think I'm going to *puke*. That was practically *pornographic*. Don't they realize there's a spy-cam in there? This is a rehab hospital, not a truck stop!"

Aunt George laughed. "Don't be such a prude, Theresa. Besides, they're both adults."

"They're *divorced*!"

Lucy opened the door a few moments later looking flushed. She beckoned to me. "Come on back in."

"Is the tonsil hockey over, or just in halftime?"

Lucy laughed, thinking I'd made a joke.

Mel was plunked on the couch, grinning like he knew some fabulous secret.

Aunt George excused herself to run for pies she'd forgotten on the back seat of the Expedition.

I followed Lucy into the kitchen alcove to check on the turkey.

"You okay?" she asked, noting my stern expression.

"Just fine," I lied. I was confused. Mel *knew* Lucy, obviously had strong feelings for her, but seemed totally oblivious that the last thing he'd told her was, "Get your cheating ass out of my house and never come back."

"I'm sorry if we embarrassed you, Theresa," Lucy grinned.

That did it. "I'm not embarrassed, *Mom*," I hissed. "So what if my divorced parents were sucking face like a pair of horny chimps? So what if you're taking advantage of a man who thinks he's still married to you, who doesn't remember you're a…an *adulterer*! You cheated on Mel. You slept with creepy Harold, your fat boss! Don't you dare hurt Mel again, Lucy! Don't you dare!"

Tears sprung to Lucy's eyes.

"Don't *you* dare speak to your mother that way again, Theresa-Jean! Ever! Do you understand?" The words were slow and slurred, but the tone meant business.

*"Dad?"* I whipped around to face Mel who was lurching towards me with the cane.

"Theresa, you've been very patient with me these past few months. I know how much my memory loss must have hurt and confused you. But I'm back and I'm telling you to show your mother some respect!"

Lucy sniffed and set the oven mitts aside. "I'll go help Georgina with the pies."

*"Dad?"* I was crying, shaking, so amazed that Mel was suddenly himself, so ashamed he'd witnessed my latest tirade. "You mean…you were trying to tell me…"

Mel nodded, took my hand, and led me back to the couch. We sat and Mel took a long, deep breath. "I woke up yesterday from an afternoon nap wondering what the hell I was doing in a hospital bed. I was terrified, wondering where you were, if someone had been called in to cover my classes, why my legs felt so weak. Then, like waves crashing onto the shore, over the course of a half-hour, everything came back. *Everything.* The good, the bad, the ugly, *and* the divorce. And remarkably, a lot of insight into all of those things. Shows you what a good bop in the head can do for you," he chuckled.

"But how…"

"The doctors say this can happen with retrograde amnesia. It's not uncommon for head-injury patients to suddenly regain their long-term memory once their brains have had enough time to heal. They tell me my case was pretty severe though, that I'm really very lucky to have made this kind of progress."

I'm very lucky you did, too, I thought.

"I called Georgie last night," he continued. "She confirmed you'd been staying at The Cabin with her, said you'd just left for a school dance. She wanted me to call your cell phone, but I didn't want to spoil your hot date."

"As if."

"I told her I'd wait and surprise you with the news today."

So that's why Aunt George was still awake and dancing around the house when I got in. And here I thought she'd just spent a good night hammering out kinks in her latest manuscript.

Mel wasn't done. "And I called Lucy. We talked for hours and hours."

"Considering that smutty kiss you gave her, she must have laid out quite the apology," I remarked.

"I had some apologizing to do, myself," Mel replied.

"Why?" I asked. "You never cheated." Then I reconsidered. *"Did you?"*

"I cheated your mother out of the partnership our marriage could and should have been. I cheated *you*, Theresa-Jean, out of a strong mother-influence growing up. I cheated myself by giving up the love of my life without a fight."

"I've been trying to get along better with Lucy," I said, knowing full well that actions spoke louder than words.

Mel grinned. "I'd say the three of us have a ways to go before anyone asks us to pose for the cover of *Family Life Magazine*," he said, pulling me into a close hug.

I breathed in the familiar scent of his wool sweater. Mel—*my* Mel—was back! "I can't believe it!" I cried into his shoulder as he held me tight. In terms of his speech and motor skills, Mel wasn't a hundred per cent, but reclaiming his memory was Capital-P Progress, something to be truly thankful for that Thanksgiving.

We were just getting started on the pumpkin pie when a doctor appeared in the doorway. "Come on in, Dr. Max," Mel gestured. "Help yourself to some pie."

"Thanks," Dr. Max said, cutting a mega-slice. "Pumpkin pie counts as a vegetable serving, doesn't it?" He winked at me.

Mel introduced us all, then Dr. Max said, his mouth full of pie, "Well, Mel, it looks like you won't be able to go home for a Christmas visit after all."

I was set to protest, but Dr. Max winked at me again.

He grinned at Mel. "We'll be sending you home for good December eighteenth. Of course, you'll still need weekly out-patient therapy for some time, but we're all delighted at your enormous progress. This time next year, you should be good as new and back to work. Congratulations!" He pumped Mel's hand.

After the doctor left, Mel, Lucy and Aunt George drank coffee and talked excitedly about the future. I was too bewildered to speak. Things were moving so fast, too fast. Mel kept sliding his hand up and down Lucy's thigh under the table and making disgusting goo-goo eyes at her. He'd actually gotten down on his rickety knees during the salad course and asked Lucy to remarry him. And she'd said yes, just like that, without a moment's hesitation, and started talking about selling the condo and requesting a job transfer to the Ottawa Y like she'd been planning it all along.

Regarding Mel's discharge from the Centre, Aunt George suggested that instead of returning to the bungalow in town, we could all share The Cabin indefinitely. "There's plenty of room and you wouldn't have to go to the Centre for your weekly physio. We could hire someone to come to the house. The pool and exercise equipment are already there."

Mel said thanks but no thanks. He preferred to settle back in town, at home, his own home. He could hire someone to make whatever renovations might be necessary.

"How do you feel about all this, Theresa?" Mel asked.

I took a deep breath. I didn't want to spoil the party mood and voice my big fear: that Mel might relapse. Not unlike Ethan with his CF readings, I'd spent time on the Internet researching amnesia. It was unlikely—but possible—that Mel could go for another nap tomorrow and wake up in la-la-land all over again.

"You have to do what will make you happy, Dad," I said. "I'll be off to university in less than a year." With the exception of the early-start program in B.C. I'd applied to last spring when my life seemed so simple and stress-free, I'd been procrastinating with my university applications. Since Mel's injury, my main concern had been keeping myself available to help with his therapies. It seemed logical then, but with Mel doing better and Lucy planning to move back to North Creek, I wondered if it was now more logical to clear out ASAP and give the born-again lovebirds a little space. I loved logic, understood it, sought comfort from it. Feelings were another matter altogether.

"Still planning to study Zoology?" Lucy asked. "Save the wolves and polar bears and everything?"

"No, I was thinking of becoming a family therapist."

"Very funny," Lucy grinned. Before dinner, I'd apologized for my blow-up about Harold and the snide comments I'd made about the over-enthusiastic way she'd responded to Mel. Lucy assured me that she would never have kissed him like that if they hadn't already reconciled. "I know you'd never believe it, but I do have one or two scruples, Theresa. Your mother's not a saint, but she's not a psycho-bitch either," she'd said. Now there was a self-actualized statement if I'd ever heard one.

"But seriously," Lucy said now. "I know you'll be finished your high school credits in December. I was just curious about what comes next."

I shrugged. "I talked to Dr. Kremp at the Animal Hospital last week when I brought Harley in to be spayed; she may be able to arrange some volunteer work for me. Or I guess there's still the possibility I'll get into the B.C. program; I'd start university classes this coming January, then come back home for a few weeks in June for my North Creek graduation. In any case, I'll be out of your hair by next September. I'm pretty sure Guelph or McMaster will take me."

Mel seemed perplexed at the mention of my graduation. "Theresa?" he asked. "Where's the canoe?"

"In Aunt George's shed," I said, trying not to display the emotion I felt. The canoe had been Mel's pride and joy. Since July it had been perched upside-down over two saw-horses, still unfinished and collecting dust. But there was no way I had forgotten our planned trip.

"Give it away," Mel said with finality. "My hands are too weak now to finish it. My canoeing days are over."

"But—" I couldn't believe what I was hearing. I wanted to tell Mel that lots of disabled people went canoeing; I'd researched that, too. There were adapted paddles and special backrests, and if all else failed, I was strong enough to paddle for two.

Mel cut me off. "We'll find some other special way to celebrate your graduation. Would it be okay if Lucy celebrated with us?"

"Sure," I said, trying to hide my disappointment, determined to find some way over the next few months to change his mind. The new Mel was going to take some getting used to.

I'd fantasized a billion times over the past few months what it would be like when Mel gained back his memories, but I'd never counted on all this. I just figured he and I would go back to the little bungalow in town and life would go on like before. But if things changed when Mel was injured, they were more changed now. And without a doubt, they'd keep changing. And so would I, whether I liked it or not.

# Chapter 10

The next morning, Lucy and Aunt George went back to the Centre to go over the details of Mel's pre-Christmas discharge. I opted to stay home and sleep in. I'd promised Mel I would be in to visit the following afternoon, Thanksgiving Day, and bring a stack of the recent issues of science journals he hadn't gotten around to, what with his being off at Hogwarts and all.

Admittedly, I was looking forward to having him to myself; I still wasn't completely comfortable sharing my father's affection with Lucy. This "thing" between my parents was too new and quite frankly, too *bizarre* for me to trust it would last. I wished them the best, but I was familiar with the laws of probability; I wasn't about to bet my bottom dollar on happily-ever-after. Lucy and Mel, in the throes of planning a sappy Valentine's wedding, felt differently. I was planning to come down with one of Ethan's handy stomach viruses that day. Let them dress up Harley as maid of honour.

Lucy was leaving for Toronto from the Centre—she had to work the statutory holiday—so we'd already said our goodbyes. She would be back the following weekend, she'd said, and every weekend until Mel's discharge. By then, Lucy hoped her job transfer would be approved and she could begin the next chapter of her life in North Creek. By then, I hoped I'd have dibs on a life as far away from North Creek as possible.

I didn't mean that, not really. When I left for university, whether in January or September, I would miss my parents, or at least I'd miss Mel and Lucy separately; it was the two of them together that ignited my flight instincts. If they really wanted to reunite, I didn't trust myself not to mess it up for them. I was an old pro at being Mel's daughter, and I was learning, slowly, to be Lucy's daughter, but I had no idea how to be *their* daughter. No wonder Dr. Spellman had such a nice car; he got rich off the stress and confusion of people like Lucy, Mel and I, people who's family ties were frayed, twisted in knots, and ready to trip them up at the first misstep.

I didn't get to sleep in. The phone began ringing a half-hour after Lucy and Aunt George left for the Centre. I thought we'd agreed to keep Mel's recovery to ourselves until Tuesday so we'd have a little time with him over the long weekend before he was besieged by old friends, colleagues, and lawyers. But Aunt George or Lucy must have let something slip when they stopped in town for gas because by mid-morning, it seemed the whole town of three-thousand had called asking for news about Mel. It pissed me off. Where were all these well-wishers when Mel was in a coma and not expected to live? Where were they when Mel was first sent to the Centre, mumbling and unable to feed himself? Mr. Harnett, who'd been there through the thick and the thin and the just plain horrible, was the only person who deserved the full scoop.

Public relations work was no picnic; by noon I needed a breather. I took Harley for an hour-long run by the river, swam fifty lengths in the lap pool, and took a long, hot shower. Then I set out west on the highway towards Smiths Falls in search of anonymity and an open library. I had a research paper due for Geography, and the essay portions of my fall-entrance university applications were due at the end of the month. There was no point procrastinating a day longer. I had no idea what the next few months would bring, but I had every reason to want to keep my options open.

I left Smiths Falls at five o'clock with my university essays polished and my ten-page paper discussing the implications of global warming on the Western Cordillera region ready to print. Hungry and brain-cramped, I devoured some chicken fingers and a large Coke at KFC and set off towards home along the scenic route. I was in no rush. Aunt George wouldn't be home before eight and I didn't relish the thought of having to field more nosy phone calls.

I wasn't far from Ethan's house when I noticed two bundles of yellow fur scuttling back and forth across the dusty road. I braked a hair short of hitting one and dashed out after them.

"Hey, boys!" I bent down and called the puppies to me. "Ernie? Bert? What are you fellows doing on the road?" They wouldn't have lasted long out there; if a passing semi didn't flatten them they'd have been dinner for roaming coyotes.

"Let's get you home, guys." I lifted the tiny retrievers into the Jeep and drove another hundred metres down the road to the Stinson's. I was surprised to see Ethan's truck in the driveway, but shrugged it off; one of his parents might have driven him to the airport to save on overnight parking fees. But then I remembered Ethan mentioning that Ellie and his parents were going to Kingston for a weekend CF fundraiser, and that Ernie and Bert would be boarding at Josie's Kennels in town. This would explain the absence of the Stinson's mini-van, but wouldn't explain why the puppies, with their matching blue collars, were out playing unsupervised on the dark rural road. I wasn't in the mood to play Nancy Drew; Aunt George was the sleuth of the family.

The Stinson house was dark but for a light in the kitchen. Hoisting the puppies up in one arm, I rang the bell and waited. If no one was home, I'd take the two furballs home with me for the night. Harley would be thrilled to play hostess.

I was just turning to leave when the door was flung open. I was shocked to see Ethan there, shirtless and dressed in grubby grey sweatpants. He hadn't shaved, his hair was wild, his eyes were red-rimmed, and he looked pale and confused and not at all pleased to see me.

"Tee?" He squinted. Without his glasses, he looked different, unfamiliar.

I set the puppies down in the foyer. "I was on my way home from Smiths Falls and saw Ernie and Bert playing out on the road. I wanted to make sure they got home safe."

"Thanks." Ethan's voice was a dull monotone. "I put them in the fenced area out back a while ago. Guess I didn't latch the gate properly."

"You haven't left for Newfoundland yet? Or are you back already?" I asked, not knowing how to acknowledge his presence, not sure that I should.

"I didn't go. I'm not going." Same dull monotone.

I raised a brow and waited to see if he'd explain. I didn't want to pry, but Ethan seemed very out of it. His eyes stared off, unfocused.

Ethan sighed deeply. "Tina called me early yesterday morning, about a half-hour before I was supposed to leave for the airport. Told me not to come. Broke up with me. She's seeing Doug Jacobs, my old next-door-neighbour. He's in college. Plays junior hockey. Has nice ears. They've been together for three weeks. *Three weeks!* Tina didn't tell me sooner because she 'didn't want to hurt me if it turned out to be just a fling.'"

That's gotta hurt, I thought. "What about her big plans for the future?"

Ethan's voice was bitter. "Tina's plan is rock solid; I guess any guy will do…so long as she ends up with a white picket fence in the suburbs." Ethan slouched against the door frame. "I'm such an idiot."

I was still trying to make sense of it all. "What about all those phone calls? Why was she checking up on you so often if she'd started seeing another guy?"

"I don't know. Maybe she was just trying to piss me off so I'd break up with her first. Save her the trouble of having to do it." His words had begun to slur. My eyes were drawn to an empty liquor bottle on the kitchen table.

"Are you *drunk*?" I asked incredulously.

"Hell, yeah. My parents and Ellie left for Kingston yesterday afternoon. Ellie asked if I wanted to come with them, seeing I was so bummed out and all. But I'm not in the mood for a fundraiser; that would take enthusiasm, which I'm lacking right now. So I agreed to stay home with the puppies. But according to you, they almost got run over." He laughed cheerlessly. "Am I on a roll or what?" He gestured to the bottle on the counter. "Newfoundland Screech. It was sent to my dad from a neighbour back home. My parents don't drink much. I never did…" Ethan rambled.

"I better get going," I said.

"Please stay," Ethan said.

"No, I should get home," I replied. Since Mel's accident I'd stopped thinking drunk people were funny. I'd stopped going to parties where I knew beer would be the only beverage. I'd pretty much stopped going to parties altogether.

"But, Tee, don't you understand?" Ethan's eyes lit up. "We can be together, now," He hugged me, pinning me against the door. He reeked of alcohol.

"Not now, Ethan. Not while—"

He kissed me. A sloppy, rum-flavoured kiss that made me gag.

"*Ethan!*" I tried to push him away, but he was bigger and stronger and way too horny to listen to reason.

"Come on, Tee. Be a friend." Ethan unzipped my jacket and reached a cold hand under my sweater.

"*Back off, Ethan!*" I squirmed as his hand found its way inside my bra. With his other hand he started fumbling with the ties of my drawstring pants.

"*Stop it, Ethan! NOW!*"

He didn't hear me. "Tee, I've wanted this for so long, since the first day I met you and you laughed at my dumb joke in English class. You're so soft," he murmured into my neck, running a hand up my thigh.

I glanced down. Ethan's sweatpants were bunched around his ankles. If I didn't stop him now...

"*GET THE HELL AWAY FROM ME!*" I screamed and brought my knee up hard into Ethan's groin.

"*SHIT!*" he yelled and backed away. "What did you do that for? I thought—"

I pulled my clothes together quickly and ran through the front door, hot angry tears running down my cheeks.

"Tee, wait! Come back! Please! I'm so sorry." Ethan stumbled down the porch stairs after me as I ran to the Jeep.

I heard a crash and turned to see Ethan on the ground. He moaned and got up on his knees, threw up violently and passed out, right there in a pile of vomit and leaves at the bottom of the porch steps. Inside, the puppies barked in confusion.

My common sense was pulling me towards the Jeep. Just get yourself out of there, Tee, my logical self was saying. But then this weird compassionate self began worrying whether Ethan would freeze to death if I left him out there, half-naked in the five Celsius weather. Or what if he threw up again and choked to death?

Ethan was too weak to put up a fight. He let me help him back up the stairs and into the house. I put the puppies in their crate with food, water, and a few chew toys and led Ethan to the bathroom. I helped him out of his barfy sweatpants, ran a warm bath, and dumped in a half-bottle of pink, rose-scented bubble bath I found in the cabinet.

I took Ethan's dirty clothes downstairs to the washer, then bounded back up and sat on the toilet lid while Ethan soaked and moaned. I didn't want to be there, but I didn't want him to drown either, if he passed out again.

After fifteen minutes, I washed his sticky hair, drained the tub, and passed him the towels and clean boxers I found in the bedroom I figured was his. I made him down two Tylenols with a large glass of water and put him to bed.

"Want me to read you a story, too?" I asked, still irritated. Playing nursemaid was exhausting work.

Ethan didn't respond. He was already asleep.

# Chapter 11

Harley was downstairs barking her happy brains out a little after eight the next morning. I groaned and rolled over in bed, wishing the flannel sheets could buffer me from the world a little longer.

"Tee?" Aunt George rapped on my door and peeked into my room. "Your friend Ethan is downstairs. Says he needs to talk to you."

"I'm sleeping."

"He seems a little upset."

"I'll bet." I threw back the covers. Let's get this over with, I thought.

I threw on a pair of jeans and a sweater and trudged downstairs. "Hey," I said to Ethan, who'd been invited by Aunt George to sit on the couch. I passed him, padded into the kitchen, and returned with two mugs of black coffee. "They're both for you," I said, setting them on the end table.

Ethan lifted a mug, took a long sip, then asked, "Could we go for a walk, Tee, please? I need to talk to you. I want to apologize for last night."

"Yeah." I grabbed my jacket and led Ethan through Aunt George's backyard to the dock. Mist rose peacefully from the river in the early morning sun. I wasn't furious with Ethan anymore, just bitterly disappointed he wasn't the guy I thought he was. Maybe I was someone who would always have bad luck with men. Maybe I'd end up like Aunt George, give up on the male species altogether and write murder mysteries to quell my frustrations.

"How do you feel this morning?" I asked Ethan. He'd stretched out flat on the dock and was staring at the marshmallow clouds overhead.

He sighed and turned his head towards me. His eyes were red and sleepy, his face was pale, but he'd shaved and smelled okay. "I feel like crap, Tee, on *so* many levels. I'm so sorry."

Sitting cross-legged a few feet away, I tossed a rock out into the river and watched the ripples fan across the narrow channel. "Ethan, do you even remember what happened?" I asked. "You were pretty ripped."

Ethan took a deep breath. "What I do remember is pretty bad." He was silent for a few seconds, then continued, "I'm not a drinker, Tee. Believe it or not, I had never drunk alcohol, not even beer, until last night. I was just so angry at Tina. I felt like such a tool for going along with her stupid 'plan' when I knew it would never work, knew that I was starting to have feelings for—" He stopped, pushed his hair behind his ear. "The Screech was just sitting there going to waste and I thought it might help me sleep, make me forget." He paused again. "You must hate me now."

I shook my head. "I don't hate you, Ethan. But it'll sure be a long while before I'll want to kiss you again."

Ethan groaned in embarrassment. He sat up and turned to me. "Tee, please don't think last night is how I operate: coming on like a bulldozer, not knowing when to stop, not taking no for an answer. I'm really so sorry."

I hurled another rock into the river, then turned to him. "You scared me last night, Ethan. I didn't want my first time to be with some pushy, horny drunk on the rebound. And you know how I feel about alcohol. My father was nearly killed by a drunk driver."

Ethan sat up, looked me in the eye. "I am never going to drink like that again, Tee. I hurt you, my stomach is reeling, my head feels like it's stuffed with cotton balls. Dammit, I'm such a jerk."

I didn't want him to think what he did was okay, but I was tired and wanted to get past it. "Ethan, why don't you come to the city with me today? I want you to meet Mel. I didn't get a chance to tell you last night, but he regained his memory." I couldn't help but grin.

Ethan's eyes brightened. "That's *awesome* news, Tee! I'm so happy for you!" He reached out as if to hug me, then thought better of it and drew his hands back quickly, afraid to touch me now.

I ignored his discomfort. "Maybe after visiting hours we could go see the new Bond flick or something," I suggested. "I haven't been to a movie in months."

Ethan nodded, seeming grateful that I'd more or less accepted his apology. "I'd like that." He grew serious again. "Any possibility we could just start over, Tee? Pretend last night never happened?"

I shook my head. "Not a chance. But you've really been there for me these past few weeks, Ethan. I don't want to write off our friendship entirely or make you feel bad forever, but I'm going to need some time. To trust you again. We can keep going from here."

"*Here* is pretty uncomfortable," Ethan said.

"Of course it is. We've only known each other six weeks, but I've seen you naked and covered in puke, and you've touched me in places and ways that made me wonder if under your wouldn't-hurt-a-fly exterior you were really a rapist. But that was yesterday. Let's make today better."

I'd been worried about how Mel would react to Ethan, with his long hair and farm hand's physique. Unlike some seventeen-year-old guys, like Joey, who were still all arms and legs and peach fuzz, Ethan looked older, more filled out. But they hit it off, Mel asking a million questions about Newfoundland's ecosystems and Ethan letting him win, but only by a hair, a game of chess. Very smooth, I thought, especially for a self-proclaimed geek.

Periodically, Mel would catch my eye and wink. If he'd known the history of the small bruise on my left breast or of Ethan's sore groin, he'd have impaled Wonderboy on his four pronged cane, but the theme of the visit was "accentuate the positive," and so far so good.

After the chess game, Mel sent Ethan to the snack bar for Cokes so he and I could have a few minutes alone.

"Well, Theresa-Jean," Mel said, his voice still slow and slurred despite his obvious alertness. "I know I don't need to give you a lecture on the birds and the bees, or even the primates, but—"

"Ethan and I are just buddies."

Mel looked up at the ceiling tiles. "God," he said. "Finally, my Theresa meets a smart boy, one who can almost whip my ass at chess, a guy who doesn't mind visiting her crippled old man in rehab, and she tells me they're 'just buddies.'" Mel shifted his gaze to me. "What's wrong with him? Is he gay?"

I didn't want to get into explanations, but that's how it was with Mel: he wouldn't let up about something until he

knew the 5 W's of everything. It was the part of him I
didn't miss when his biggest concern was learning to use a
fork again.

"No," I sighed. "He's not gay. Ethan's girlfriend back
home dumped him over the phone Saturday morning and
he had a bad time of it yesterday. His family is in Kingston
for the weekend, and I just thought it would be—"

Mel interrupted, "By 'bad time of it,' you mean?"

"He finished off a twenty-sixer of Screech last night,"
I said.

Mel smirked. "Weird, Ethan doesn't strike me as the
party-boy type."

I shook my head. "He's not. He was just upset and
alone, and the bottle was there."

"And you know this because?"

Time to fudge the details. "I stopped by his house last
night to ask him about a chemistry assignment and found
him pretty wasted. I put him to bed and came home. He
dropped by Aunt George's this morning to apologize, so I
invited him to tag along today. Thought it might coax him
out of his funk."

Mel rolled his eyes. "And no doubt to present me as a
public service announcement, as a victim of the perils of
drunken senselessness. You should have brought him a
few weeks ago when I was drooling and having trouble
strategizing tic-tac-toe."

I let it go. "Dad, Ethan and I are going to see the new
Bond movie this evening. Want to come with us? I asked at
the desk if it would be okay to kidnap you for a few hours.
We can fold the wheelchair into the back of the Jeep."

Mel grinned. "I'd love to blow this joint for awhile, but
I'm wiped, kid. Too much excitement this weekend. And
tomorrow it'll be therapy out the wazoo as usual. Could we

go somewhere next weekend instead? With Lucy?"

"Sure, Dad." He did look worn out, though his cheeks were still rosy and his eyes bright.

As I reached for my jacket, my eyes fell on a slip of paper on Mel's dresser. Under the Centre letterhead was typed yesterday's date and "Reservation: Rm B-04." I knew "B" stood for Basement. And I knew that for in-patients who were well enough to have overnight guests, there were several conjugal apartments in the basement that could be booked nightly like hotel rooms. The rooms were jokingly referred to as the "Jungle Suites" by the staff.

Mel noticed my shift in attention. He laughed loudly. "Do you really want to know?"

Oh, gross, I thought. That's why Mel was worn out. They really did it. Mel and Lucy together in an adjustable hospital bed was a thought best reserved for an empty stomach.

"No," I blushed. "Definitely not."

On the way to the Cineplex, I told Ethan about my parents' weird reunion. How Mel's open affection for Lucy was so different from the yelling and silences of my childhood. How I was afraid it wouldn't last, that someone was going to get hurt again. How I just knew that someone would be me.

"They're adults, Tee," Ethan echoed Aunt George's earlier sentiments.

I smirked. "Technically, Ethan, you and I will both be 'adults' in less than a year. Adults can screw up pretty bad."

Ethan nodded. "Then maybe we should all just cut each other a little slack."

The movie was a blessed escape from reality, the only distraction being Ethan's proximity in the dark. I knew Ethan could feel it, too: he'd jump a little and apologize each time our legs or arms accidentally bumped. This unnerved me. I didn't want him to think he couldn't touch me at all. I just wanted him to know my body wasn't a salad bar; he couldn't just help himself to whatever and however much he pleased. I'd discovered much the previous night. One: Ethan wasn't upset about breaking up with Tina, only upset he'd been made a fool of. Two: he'd had feelings for me for some time. Three: despite his book smarts and wise theories, he, like me, had trouble dealing with strong emotions.

As I watched 007 square off against a trio of leather-clad female assassins, I convinced myself that Ethan's actions the previous night had been a combination of alcohol and acute frustration. It was our actions today, tomorrow, and in the weeks to come that would determine if we'd get another chance to turn our fledgling friendship up a notch.

I decided to test the waters. I hooked my baby finger around Ethan's. I didn't want to hold hands. I didn't want to be romantic. I just wanted to convey I hadn't written him off. We sat like that, through the closing credits, then went out for pizza and talked about easy stuff: the movie, school, books. Turned out Ethan, like Mel, was a Pat Conroy fan. Though I doubted Newfoundland farm boys had much in common with South Carolina military boys, I could see a little of Ethan in Conroy's smart, funny, fallible lead characters. And as repulsed as I'd been the night before, there was something else about Ethan. Something good that had less to do with his character than with what Mr. Harnett meant by "chemistry." It was that *ping, ping, ping,* that steady current that flowed between us like a river, now complete with raging rapids, thick marshes and sharp bends.

That got me thinking. I pulled the Jeep into Aunt George's drive a little after midnight and walked Ethan over to the turnaround where he'd left his truck that morning. I asked, "Ethan, do you do woodwork?"

"I'm a guy, aren't I?"

Oh brother. "What kinds of woodwork have you done?"

Ethan shrugged. "Porches, fences, decks, simple furniture, sheds. Back home, I helped my friend Jason fix up an old boat, a twenty-foot cruiser we found swamped in a cove in St. George's Bay."

Bingo. "If someone gave you the plans and the materials, could you build a canoe? Or more specifically, help me *finish* a canoe?"

Ethan shrugged again. "Sure."

I gestured for Ethan to follow me out back to the shed. "Let me show you something."

I swung open the shed doors and, for the first time in months, observed my father's dream with hope, not anger or sadness.

"Tee, she's beautiful."

"Could we finish it before Christmas?" I asked hopefully.

"Probably. You know I work most weekends, but weeknights aren't too busy once my chores and homework are done."

"I want to finish it for Mel. He and I got it this far, but I can't finish it alone; I have ten thumbs when it comes to building things. Mel mostly had me hold stuff, pass him tools, read instructions out loud."

"Will your dad mind me working on it? It's his baby, after all. Maybe someday he'll want to finish it himself."

I shook my head. "He claims his hands are no good now; his strength and fine motor skills are shot. He told me to get rid of it." Without warning, my voice began to shake. "See, the canoe was his dream and we had a little expedition planned for my graduation this spring. I still want to go, for Mel's sake, even if I have to rig up a motor or do most of the paddling myself. I want to surprise him at Christmas when he comes home. The trip will give him incentive to keep up with his out-patient therapy." I shut the shed door and walked Ethan back to his truck.

He opened the driver's door and turned back to me. "Again, Tee, I'm so sorry about last night."

I laid a hand on his shoulder. "Don't sweat it. Go home. Keep the puppies off the road. Get some sleep. Call me if you get upset about Tina and want to talk."

"Okay," he said quietly. "Thanks, Tee, for everything. For rescuing Ernie and Bert. For the movie and the chance to meet your father. For not just telling me to piss off this morning."

"Thank you, too, Ethan." I said.

"What for?"

"For agreeing to work on the canoe. For coming over this morning to apologize; it took guts and it made things better. And for being cool with Mel; he's usually a hard sell in the guy department. He used to call Joey 'The Goofball' behind his back. He likes you."

Ethan raised a brow and started Wilma's ignition. "He wouldn't if he knew—"

I interrupted. "Well, he doesn't. And he won't if it never happens again."

"It won't. I *swear*, Tee—"

I grinned. "If it does, don't be surprised if Mel boils you down to the bones and donates your skeleton to the Biology department at the college."

Finally Ethan let out a laugh, his first of the day. "I don't doubt it."

# Part 3

*Take everything as it comes; the wave passes, deal with the next one.*

– Tom Thomson

# Chapter 12

Tuesday of the following week, just after lunch, Mr. Harnett came to Geography and beckoned me out of class.

"Bring your books," he said, his face grim.

What happened? I didn't think I was in trouble. Did Aunt George want me home? Why hadn't she just called my cell? Did Mel relapse? Did Mel *die*? My heart began to pound like a jackhammer. That would explain why Mr. Harnett looked so upset. What else could it be?

*Oh, God, please not Mel.*

"What is it?" I asked Mr. Harnett, trying to disguise my worry, failing miserably.

Mr. Harnett said nothing, just gave me a tortured look and gestured for me to follow him.

He steered me into the guidance office and led me to a small conference room. The door closed behind us. I glanced around, overcome by gut-wrenching terror. Police Chief Wilkins was there, looking out the window, his brow creased with anguish. And so was Ed Green, chief of the North Creek Fire Department.

Mr. Harnett motioned for me to sit.

I was close to panic. Couldn't sit. Began pacing instead. "What is it?" I repeated. "Is it Mel?"

Mr. Harnett said, "No, not Mel, but—"

"Then *what*?" I reeled around to face him.

"Theresa, your aunt's house burned down this morning."

"No," I said, not understanding. "I was home this morning. The house was fine. I made eggs for breakfast. But I turned the stove off—I'm sure of it. Aunt George was home, too. She was in the upstairs office, printing a new draft of her novel. Harley was with her, asleep beside the filing cabinets." I was blathering, not ready to face the answer to the question I had yet to ask, the answer I already knew. "Aunt George got out, right? *Right*?"

Mr. Harnett's face drained of colour. He shook his head. "She's gone, Tee. The dog, too. The smoke was just too thick."

The room was spinning. I sat, finally, to keep from falling, and put my head between my knees to keep from passing out.

Ed spoke up. "I'm sorry, Theresa. The flames began in the basement and the smoke spread quickly. Georgina managed to call 911, but by the time we got out to The Cabin it was too late. She didn't make it down the stairs."

Several long minutes passed. Someone put a gentle hand on my shoulder.

I raised my head and addressed the room, my voice barely a whisper. "How did this happen?" Then louder, *"How?"*

Chief Wilkins looked over at Mr. Harnett, raising a brow. Mr. Harnett nodded. Chief Wilkins sighed deeply. "There needs to be a full investigation, but it looks like arson. We found another body in the basement and a ten-litre gas can nearby. Dental records will have to confirm the identity—the face and hands were badly burned—but you should know Carl Smythe ran away from his detention home Sunday night. We found his wallet on the body."

I swallowed hard, trying to contain the bile rising in my

throat. Aunt George had a ten-litre gas can for the lawn mower and snow blower. Had Carl been hiding in the shed that morning? I was suddenly furious at my aunt. Why had she been so stubborn? *Damn her* for refusing to set up those high-powered security locks and electronic fences.

"How did Carl escape detention?" Mr. Harnett asked, his voice hoarse with anger.

"Reports say he slipped out undetected," Chief Wilkins said. "Riverview was short-staffed due to recent turnover. Carl probably hiked to North Creek along the river, then camped in the woods by The Cabin. By the looks of it, he broke into the house through the basement, spilled gas around, then dropped a match. Who knows if Carl wanted to die, too, or if he was just too damn stupid to consider his own escape route. There will be a full investigation, you can be sure of it."

It still didn't make any sense. "Why...Why Aunt George?" I cried. My nose was running. Mr. Harnett passed me a tissue. *"Why?"*

Chief Wilkins rubbed his hands over his face, clearly stressed. "We called Riverview this morning. Carl's primary worker remembered Carl boasting that he wanted to be his brother's 'avenger,' that when he got out he was going to 'pull something off' that would make him a household name. But Carl was always bragging about something, the worker said, so it was dismissed as hot air. Riverview never reported the threats. They never realized Carl had access to a celebrity. If we'd known, Theresa, I swear to God, we would have informed Georgina. We would have stationed guards around The Cabin until Carl was located—"

*"I hope he's burning in hell!"* I screamed suddenly, my shock morphing into white-hot rage. I couldn't believe it.

Small-town Carl with the small-time brain was going to make the cover of tabloids all over the globe. He was going down in history, not as a juvenile drug dealer and badass punk, but as an arsonist and the murderer of Georgina Simmons, best-selling author. My aunt.

Another long minute passed.

"How did Mel take it?" I asked, sick with fear.

Mr. Harnett shook his head. "He doesn't know yet. But I called Lucy right before I took you from class—she's on her way."

I freaked. "I need to see him. *Now!* We can't let Mel find out about this on the news!" I was hysterical now, hyper-ventilating, out of my seat, making a play for the door.

Mr. Harnett grabbed my shoulders and held me steady. "Mrs. Green can cover my last period class. I'll take you in my Honda."

I didn't answer. I broke free and dashed to my locker for my coat and belongings. I smacked right into Ethan, who was gathering books for his next class.

"Hey, Miss Tee, where's the fire?" he laughed, then saw my face. "Tee, what's wrong? *What happened?*"

With words interspersed with choking sobs, I barely managed to tell him the whole story.

The no-touch policy evaporated. Ethan wrapped his arms around me and kissed my hair. I was too distraught to feel the *ping, ping, ping*, but I did feel his warmth, and for just a few seconds my breathing slowed and I was able to catch my breath.

"I have to run," I said, forcing myself to let go.

"Call me, Tee. Let me know if you need anything. Or if I can do anything to help."

But I could no longer hear him. All I wanted right then was for the nightmare that was my life to end.

I feared that hearing the details of Aunt George's tragic death would send Mel back into the fog, but he was okay—angry and full of questions no one had answers for, but okay. Lucy and I stayed with him all evening while Mr. Harnett took care of the media vultures outside.

Eventually, sorrow gave way to irritability. A despondent Dr. Max gave Mel some pills to help him sleep and suggested Lucy and I go home and get some rest, too. I realized I no longer had Aunt George's home to go to, which started a fresh crop of tears.

Exhausted, I followed Lucy to a nearby Comfort Inn where we watched the day's horror unfold on the major TV networks. By news estimates, the fire had started shortly after nine a.m. It gave me the creeps to think Carl had been outside The Cabin waiting for me to leave for school so he could kill my kind, creative aunt and her sweet, rambunctious dog. I couldn't figure why he'd spared me, unless he knew that letting me live to see the carnage would hurt me more. Video footage showed the fire trucks waging war on the flames; a clip that would give me nightmares zoomed in on the wooden animals on the porch, once so majestic, now scorched and forlorn.

At midnight, a re-broadcast of Aunt George's "Biography" was interrupted by a special news bulletin. The cameras flashed on the county jail, where Jerry Smythe, whose trial was scheduled to begin early in the New Year, stood shaky in front of a microphone and denounced his brother's crime. Looking haggard and much older than his twenty-three years, Jerry spoke haltingly of being deeply disturbed by Carl's motivations and actions. He blamed himself for being a bad influence on Carl and for introducing him to drugs and alcohol at a young age. Now clean for almost four months, Jerry claimed he'd found Jesus and was in talks with his lawyer to change his plea to "guilty." Through tears, he reported a change of heart and claimed he owed it to our family and his mother to accept the consequences of his drunken recklessness.

"Do you think he's really changed?" I was poisoned by skepticism.

Lucy shrugged. "Even before I left North Creek, there was talk about the Smythe boys. Ask any teacher, cop, or business owner in town and they'll tell you: Jerry was a thief, a drunk, and an all-around mischief-maker from the time he was fourteen years old and his father died. But Ron Harnett says Carl was different. Even in kindergarten, he threatened other kids with scissors, stabbed class hamsters with pencil crayons, and stole lighters from teachers' purses. I'd bet he had some sort of mental illness, but Fran Smythe just turned her head if anyone suggested he needed more than a good talking to."

"Well, *nobody* has to see his ugly, *evil* face again!" I couldn't stop crying. All my tears made Lucy, who had been a rock all evening, start to cry, too. My mother came over to the bed where I was sprawled and held me until I fell asleep.

Aunt George's funeral was three days later. Only family and close friends were allowed inside the North Creek United Church. About a thousand others—fans, reporters, gossipmongers—crowded around outside in the rain.

Aunt George and Harley had, ironically, been cremated.

Their urns rested side by side on the pulpit. If anyone thought it was odd or in bad taste to include a dog in the funeral, I didn't care. It helped me believe that Aunt George, wherever she was now, wasn't alone.

Ethan arrived with Mr. Harnett. His navy suit was tight and short in the sleeves and he looked strangled in his tie. But his outfit was unimportant compared to the genuine compassion in his eyes and the sincere manner with which he expressed his sympathy to my parents.

For the majority of North Creek townspeople, this was the first they'd seen Mel since his injury. Most were able to downplay their shock at seeing Mel so thin and grey and weak, at hearing him speak so slowly, at watching him struggle with his cane down the church aisle. They realized how distraught he was at having to make his first trip home under such horrifying circumstances.

There was a small reception in the church basement afterwards. While Mel and Lucy spoke to Mr. Harnett, I steered Ethan into an empty Sunday school room. I had to say goodbye, at least for a while; Monday morning, Mel and I were returning to Toronto with Lucy. Mel, on compassionate grounds, had been discharged early from the Centre and accepted temporarily into an out-patient program at St. John's Rehabilitation Hospital, a short drive from Lucy's condo. I'd been granted permission by the North Creek School Board to finish my fall courses via e-mail; Principal Jones would arrange for me to sit for my exams at a Toronto high school. The couple renting our North Creek bungalow would be gone the first week of December so that renovations could be completed for Mel by Christmas. There were some who questioned if and even *why* we'd come back to North Creek—too many bad memories and all. But according to Mel, there was no damn way the Smythe's were going to run him out of his own home town. As for Lucy's condo, she planned to put it on the market as soon as we were settled back in North Creek.

"Will you be staying in town this weekend?" Ethan asked, a little dazed at the news of my sudden departure.

I shook my head. "Lucy and I are still in Ottawa at the Comfort Inn on Carling; it's quiet and the reporters are keeping their distance. Mel has to get things wrapped up at the Centre this weekend, make sure he has all his charts to pass on to the people at St. John's. And there's a meeting with some lawyers and insurance people about having The Cabin rebuilt. According to her will, Aunt George wants it converted into a writers' colony. Plus Lucy and I have to shop. I lost my clothes, my computer, my books." I could feel my eyes start to burn.

Ethan held me close. "I'll miss you like crazy."

I heard Mel in the hall calling my name. It was time to go.

"I'll miss you, too." I squeezed Ethan hard.

When I let go, Ethan looked like he was going to say something else, but I waved and hurried off before he could. I didn't want promises or requests or statements I wasn't ready to hear following me to Toronto. I'd be back in two months, and maybe by then I'd having my feelings for him sorted out.

I joined Lucy and Mel in the church parking lot and we said our quick goodbyes to Mr. Harnett, who'd agreed to transfer anything salvageable from Aunt George's property to his garage until we could sort through it in January. What I didn't realize at the time, having not been to see what was left of The Cabin, was that the shed out back, though singed on the outside by fly-away debris, had remained untouched inside. Mel's canoe, his dream, refused to die.

Late Sunday afternoon there was a light rap on the motel room door. I opened it without hesitating; Lucy had gone across the road to the plaza to pick up some Chinese take-out and I thought she'd forgotten her key.

"Ellie?" She was wearing a puffy white down coat that made her look like one of those little characters you make with marshmallows and toothpicks.

"Hi," she grinned.

I beckoned her in from the cold. "How did you get here?"

"I made Ethan bring me. We looked up the address in the phone book. Your Jeep's right outside so I figured this was your room."

"Where's Ethan?" I asked.

"Still in the truck. He said we shouldn't bother you, but...well...you're probably wondering why I'm here?"

I nodded.

"Here." Ellie unzipped her coat and a fluffy yellow head poked out. She handed the puppy to me gently. "It's Ernie. Ethan told me you're going to be a zoologist, and I was so sad you lost your dog. My dad says it's too much work for me to look after two puppies, so I thought you could have Ernie. He's the athletic one. He needs an owner who can take him for long runs."

I'd seen dogs in the elevator at Lucy's condo, so I knew the building was pet-friendly. And there was a big park nearby where Ernie could socialize each day with other dogs. I could see in Ellie's eyes how much it hurt her to give the puppy away, but I could also see how much she wanted me to have him. Like her big brother, she had a good heart.

"Thank you, kiddo." I gave her a hug and prayed I wouldn't cry again. Everything set me off these days—anger, sadness, confusion, even kindness. Especially kindness.

"You're welcome," Ellie wheezed. Even through the thick coat, I could feel her ribs.

Between us, Ernie gave a yelp. I laughed and pulled away.

Ellie gave Ernie a final pat on the head and a kiss on his furry cheek. "I better go. I hope when you come back to North Creek, I can see him sometimes."

"Of course, Ellie. Anytime. Listen, could you send Ethan in for a minute? I just want to say goodbye again since I have the chance."

Ellie grinned. "Are you going to kiss him?"

I had to laugh. "You think I should?"

She nodded. "Knock his socks off."

"Hi," Ethan said, seconds later. He raised a brow when he saw Ernie tearing up the motel room, zooming over and under the two double beds, humping Lucy's gym bag, and making himself at home. "Don't feel pressured about the dog, Tee. Ellie insisted it would cheer you up, but I don't know. Maybe it's too soon."

I shook my head. "No, it's perfect, Ethan. Very thoughtful. Ernie'll keep me company in the big bad city."

Ethan nodded, then asked, "Think you'll fall in love with some flashy-dressing, smooth-talking city boy?"

"I think Ernie will be my main guy for the next while."

"I meant what I said the other day, Tee," Ethan said. "I'm really going to miss you."

So much had happened it was hard to believe that less

than ten days had passed since that night Ethan had come on so strong, too strong. His drunken boorishness seemed so insignificant now, in comparison to the death and grief and sadness that had followed. So many times before and after that night, when I felt trapped in the tumultuousness of my life, Ethan had been there, offering his friendship like a life raft.

I stood on my tiptoes. "Here's something to remember me by."

Ethan was still wearing his socks when he left a few minutes later. But he was also wearing a pretty big grin. I hoped that, somewhere, Aunt George, the relentless match-maker, was grinning too.

# Chapter 13

I expected to hate living in Toronto. I expected crowds—in the malls, in the library, in the subway, on the streets—and I found them. But what surprised me was I didn't mind them. I guess when you grow up in a fishbowl of a small town the anonymity of a big-city crowd can be a welcome change. I knew the folks back in North Creek were just trying to be nice with their frequent calls and cards of sympathy, but when your life is in turmoil, you don't necessarily want to be reminded of it every ten minutes. By contrast, I could sit for hours in Toronto food courts drinking Tim Horton's coffee and doing my faxed-in algebra units without once having someone stop to ask how I was, how Mel was, how I was coping with Aunt George's death, how I was feeling about having my parents back together again. I could relax in the patient lounge at St. John's Rehabilitation Hospital waiting for Mel to finish his daily therapy appointments and never once be asked anything more challenging than "Do you have the time?" I could take Ernie to the park and talk to other dog owners about rawhide and housebreaking and hot spots without them knowing my last puppy died of smoke inhalation. Toronto was impersonal and just what I needed. A period of calm. A chance to take a deep breath, gather my resources, and prepare for a challenging, dare I say "Happy" New Year.

Mel was dealt a major blow in early November. While his cognitive skills and memory were back to normal, and according to Lucy his libido seemed to be running overtime (too much information, Mom!), his motor reflexes were still spastic and his speech remained painfully slow despite countless hours of daily therapy. No one wanted to come right out and say Mel's disabilities would be permanent, but the therapists introduced what they called an "occupational maintenance program," the goal of which was to use exercise and technology to bridge the substantial gap between Mel's previous motor skills and his current ones. The protocol included daily strength and flexibility exercises to maintain a normal range of motion and treadmill work to build his stamina. A new computer was adapted with an extra-large keyboard and touchpad that Mel could use to access the Internet. And since he could only walk short distances, a state-of-the-art electric wheelchair was ordered so Mel could get around town on his own. It wasn't his Jeep, but it cost just as much.

I think what depressed Mel the most was that he wouldn't be able to do stand-up teaching anymore. He'd always been so charismatic in front of a class. He hadn't lost his smarts or his wit, but he'd lost his fast-paced delivery. There were options, he knew. The college had already talked to him about applying for research grants. He'd been wanting to write a series of science texts for years and would finally have the time. And though he'd miss the face-to-face contact, he knew he could still teach many of his previous courses on-line. Finally, though he hated to talk about it, Aunt George had left him a rich man; he didn't have to work another day in his life if he didn't want to.

By contrast, Lucy applied for and received a transfer to the Ottawa YMCA; she was scheduled to begin in January. She was also planning to take courses part-time to become a certified personal trainer. One of her new goals was to open her own little gym in North Creek someday. She had a lot of guts, or nerve, some would say, coming back to North Creek after the "scandal" with Harold and so much time away. Even at the funeral, I caught a few of the older church ladies clucking their tongues at Lucy, no doubt painting her as the town adulteress turned opportunistic gold-digger. But Mel and I knew, and Mr. Harnett knew, that the reunion happened before the tragedy with Aunt George.

As weird as it was, Lucy's presence was probably the best therapy Mel had going for him. They spent many evenings curled in a blanket on the couch watching Lucy's old movies and planning their new life together. I was a little put out that so many of their schemes—to drive through Europe, to add a backyard pool to the house in North Creek, to take an Alaskan Cruise—didn't involve me. I'd be off to university within a year, they kept reminding me, like they were looking forward to my departure more than I was.

Though we quickly settled into a routine—Lucy had her job, Mel had his therapy, and I had my school assignments—things weren't always hunky dory. The death of Aunt George had hit us hard, and it was a while before the media coverage waned. Weeks after the fire, I still felt like crying every time I walked into a convenience store and saw one of Aunt George's last novels on the book rack. And Lucy and I, despite our efforts to bond, still had differences. Perhaps energized by Mel's newfound adoration, or perhaps because Mel and I were currently living on *her* turf, she'd started trying to exert leadership in areas she'd never had a say in before: my curfew, my chores, my shopping habits. It wasn't that I found her expectations unreasonable, but she was telling me to do and not do things I would have done or not done willingly, without being asked.

I complained to Mel one night when Lucy got called in to teach an evening fitness class and left a note tacked to the fridge reminding me to make sure the laundry was folded and Mel's dinner was put in the oven.

"Why does she leave me these stupid notes like I'm an irresponsible ten-year-old? I've never *not* done my share of the chores. Who does she think did the laundry and made dinner last year, or the year before?"

Mel laughed. "You'll have to work that out with her."

Where was my old Mel, my ally? "But—"

"Dr. Spellman says I can't get between you and Lucy anymore."

Dr. Spellman, our weekly family outing. I sighed. "I know. I was there when the munchkin said it. But I'm practically an adult, and—"

"Don't tell Lucy how mature you are, Theresa. Show her."

More psychological mumbo-jumbo. "Show her *how*?"

"For starters, stop running to me every time you have a problem with Lucy. Don't be a tattle-tale. Just take her on one-on-one. She's your parent, too."

"But she doesn't know how to be the parent of a seventeen-year-old."

"Like I said, you need to show her."

"It's hard to act mature when you're being treated like an infant."

Mel laughed and mussed my hair. "Then I guess you've got your work cut out for you, kid."

I mussed his back. "I think Dr. Spellman has you brainwashed."

I received two pieces of mail the last week of November. The first was from the university in B.C. With the fire and all its aftermath I'd forgotten about B.C. Turned out I'd been accepted to the January-start program and was expected in Vancouver a week after New Year's for course registration and orientation. I was stunned. How could I pick up and move across the country with only five weeks notice? Maybe if I had a fantasy life, or even my old one, but there was no way now; too much had happened. I mulled it over for about five minutes, then called and declined the offer. The university apologized for the lengthy time it took to forward the acceptance to my new address and told me I had until registration day to change my mind.

The second piece of mail was a Rideau Canal postcard. I felt the *ping, ping, ping* even before turning it over to see who it was from. I wondered if my feelings for Ethan had something to do with my decision to hang around North Creek a little longer than necessary, but I promptly dismissed the notion. I wasn't one of those crazy girls who gave up their own dreams for some man.

I flipped the card over.

> *Hey Miss Tee!*
>
> *I'm coming to Toronto next week. Ellie's having G-tube surgery at Sick Kids Hospital on Tuesday morning. It's supposed to be a pretty simple procedure, so I may have some spare time if all goes well.*
>
> *Want to show me the town?*
>
> *Miss you lots,*
>
> *Ethan*

I phoned Ethan for the details. Ellie needed a gastrostomy tube inserted to receive supplemental liquid nutrition at night while she slept. Despite taking huge doses of oral enzymes, her digestive system was failing and she would continue to lose weight unless her regular food intake was boosted with high-caloric liquid supplementation. The procedure could be done at the children's hospital in Ottawa, but the wait period was less if she agreed to have the surgery at Sick Kids in Toronto.

"Is she scared?" I asked Ethan.

"A little, but she knows a few kids at the Ottawa CF clinic who have had a tube inserted and knows it'll help her gain weight. It's a pretty straightforward procedure: they'll make a small incision through the abdomen into the stomach and then insert a tube that is held in place by a small water balloon. Ellie'll even learn how to replace the tube herself if it gets clogged or the balloon tears and the tube falls out at school."

"Mel had a naso-gastric tube when he was in a coma," I said.

Ethan nodded. "Same idea, but the G-tube is more cosmetic. Ellie can hide it under her shirt. Most kids at school won't even know she has it because she can still eat regular food during the day."

"How long will Ellie be in the hospital?"

"Only a few days if there are no complications. I'm going to miss a Physics test, but I've never been to Toronto, and well, like I said, I miss you. So will we be able to get together?"

Like he had to ask.

Ethan showed up on Lucy's doorstep just before noon on Tuesday, looking so great, so familiar, in his scruffy old Levi's and soft flannel shirt.

"Well, I made it!" Ethan let out a deep breath; he'd never taken a subway before.

I pulled him into the condo and gave him a first-rate hello hug. "How was the surgery?" I asked.

"Very quick. Ellie was already awake and chatting up the nurses when I left to come here. She says to say hi to you, and Ernie, of course."

Hearing his name, Ernie bounded out to the hall from his favourite spot beside Mel's easy chair. He was a little over four months now, a clumsy forty pounds, with big feet he'd soon grow into. While Lucy was more of a cat person, Ernie and my father had become best buddies. Ernie followed Mel everywhere; even when Mel was in the bathroom with the sports page, Ernie would be sprawled outside the door waiting expectantly for the flush. I didn't mind. I got Ernie to myself during the day when Mel was at St. John's. When I wasn't working on school assignments, we took long walks in the park, shopped for chew toys at PetsMart, and attended Puppy Preschool classes at a local animal clinic.

"What are the chances of smuggling Ernie into Ellie's hospital room?" Ethan asked.

Turned out the chances were nil. Ethan's cell phone rang halfway through our late lunch at The Pickle Barrel.

"Oh, God. I'll be right there." Ethan clicked the phone off and turned to me, his face grim.

His alarm was contagious. "Ethan, what's wrong?"

"Ellie's unconscious. The doctors think she may have contracted an infection during surgery. They've been pumping her full of antibiotics for the past half-hour, but she's not coming around. I have to go. Sorry, Tee." He stood up, tossing some money on the table to cover lunch.

I shook my head, also standing up. "Don't apologize, Ethan. Let me drive you to the hospital—it'll be faster."

Ethan nodded and grabbed his jacket from the back of his chair. "Thanks for understanding."

I pulled into the Emergency turnaround at Sick Kids twenty minutes later and killed the ignition. I wrapped my arms around Ethan in the passenger seat. He'd been so quiet during the ride.

"I'm so scared," he whispered into my hair.

I held him tighter. "Ethan, I hope and pray that Ellie comes around. And please, remember I'm here for you."

Ethan disentangled himself and straightened his glasses. There were tears in his eyes. "Thanks again, Tee. I'll call as soon as I know something."

I watched him hurry through the revolving door into the bustling hospital. I knew first-hand what dread felt like, in the mind, in the heart, in the pit of the stomach.

"Ellie, please be okay," I whispered over and over all the way home. Too distracted to work on school assignments, I paced Lucy's windy balcony for over an hour as, below, the early rush hour traffic snaked through the streets like a river of steel.

I was late picking Mel up from St. John's.

"You and Ethan have a fight?" he asked immediately, noting my grim expression. He'd expected Ethan to be with me and had looked forward to cajoling him into a game of chess.

Fighting back tears, I told him what happened to Ellie.

"Were you this worried about *me* when I was in the hospital?" Mel meant it in a teasing way, as if he had no idea the anguish I'd been through when he was in the hospital attached to a dozen machines and not expected to pull through.

"You don't know the half of it, Mel!" I yelled.

"Easy does it," Mel said, clearly startled by my reaction.

"You don't know the half of it," I repeated, starting to cry.

"Pull over," Mel instructed. I brought the Jeep to a stop.

He reached for my hand; I yanked it away. "Look, I'm sorry, Theresa. It's true; I don't know the half of it. But I guess it must have been hell, must *still* be hell sometimes. You've been through so much in the past six months. You lost your aunt, you almost lost me, you've had to leave your home and your school, and I know having your mother back seems like a mixed blessing at times."

I grabbed a tissue from the glove compartment and blew my nose.

"But Theresa, your marks are still top-drawer, you make time to run, you have room in your heart for your friends. You're becoming such a strong young woman, someone I'm very proud of. Just please don't lose your sense of humour."

Later that evening, while Lucy and Mel were snuggled in the den watching *Casablanca* and I was posted at the kitchen table waiting for the phone to ring, there was a rap at the door.

I checked the peephole, then threw open the door. "Ethan! I've been so worried."

He looked exhausted, but was grinning from ear to ear. "I'm sorry for not calling. I wanted to see you again and took a chance you'd be home."

"How's Ellie?"

"She'll be okay—this time, anyway. It looked pretty bad for a while. The doctors had to pull out the stops and try a new experimental antibiotic. Thank God, it worked right away. She's awake again."

"That's wonderful news!" I threw my arms around his neck.

"Tee?"

"Mmm?" I mumbled into his shirt.

"I could really use a kiss right now."

I laughed. "Or maybe several?"

Lucy walked in on us a few minutes later. "Sorry, Theresa," she giggled. "I didn't know you had company. Ethan, how is your sister?"

Ethan blushed and grabbed for his glasses on the counter. "She'll be okay. They caught the infection in time."

Lucy was cool. "Have you eaten? Would you like some leftover spaghetti?"

Ethan nodded enthusiastically and proceeded to devour a heaping plate like a hungry lion. Soon Mel tottered out to see what was taking Lucy so long in the kitchen. The four of us ended up playing Monopoly until after ten. Ethan had a way of bringing out the best in my parents. I wondered if they felt he had the same effect on me.

"Feel free to sleep on the couch," Lucy told Ethan when the game wrapped up. But Ethan explained he'd brought the minivan that evening because he needed to be back downtown by eleven to pick up his father—they'd be sharing a room at the Holiday Inn. Mrs. Stinson was staying at the hospital with Ellie.

"We'll say goodnight then." Lucy smiled at Ethan, winked at me, and pulled Mel down the hall with her to their bedroom.

"Your mother's nice," Ethan said when we were alone again. "After all the horror stories you've told me, I thought she'd chase me out with a broom when she caught us kissing."

I smirked. "Lucy's hardly in a position to criticize."

"And your dad is one mean monopoly player. Has he always been so competitive?"

I laughed. "Last Spring, Mel ran the National Capital Marathon. Three hours and twenty minutes. Not record breaking, but amazing for a first-timer. Mr. Harnett says he's still running marathons, just different ones."

I kissed Ethan for a good long while before he slipped out into the night armed with a stack of Ernie photos I'd taken recently at the park. No way with Ellie's infection could we risk sneaking the dog into her hospital room. Besides, Ethan had heard talk they might be transferring Ellie back to Ottawa the next day if she was well enough to travel.

"Theresa?" Lucy called when I passed her room on my way to bed a few minutes later.

I took a step back and popped my head in the doorway. Lucy was alone. "Mel's in the bathroom," she replied before I could ask. She gestured for me to sit on the bed.

"I like Ethan, Theresa. But take it slow." Motherly advice, like I didn't have two brain cells to rub together.

"Not all of us are ruled by our sex drives," I sniped, hoping Mel wouldn't overhear. "Ethan's sister is very sick— we've both been through a lot lately. We're becoming good friends. Don't worry about me being pressured to do anything I'm not comfortable with. I'm not a naïve fourteen-year-old, you know."

"You're using birth control?"

"Mom! This is the first I've *seen* him in weeks! So what if I kissed him? Unless I've been seriously misinformed, that won't get me pregnant."

"I just wanted to remind you, I'm here if you need…anything."

Mel came out of the bathroom laughing. "Jesus, Lucy, she's old enough to buy her own condoms." He winked at me to let me know he was just teasing.

"Dad, don't you start."

Mel put his arm around Lucy's shoulder. "Love is such a beautiful thing. Our little girl is growing up."

Oh, gag. "I'm going to bed now," I announced, rising. "Alone. With my headphones on. Again."

Lucy frowned. "Has the traffic down on Yonge Street been keeping you awake?"

"Yeah," I replied. That and the horrifying sounds of her and Mel doing the mattress mambo in the next room. Love may be a beautiful thing, but it could also be a very noisy thing.

Just before midnight, my cell phone rang. I snatched it up quickly. "Ethan?" Who else would be phoning me at that hour?

"Tee. I'm sorry for calling so late."

"I wasn't asleep yet. Is everything okay?" My stomach lurched. Had Ellie relapsed?

"Something happened to me tonight when I stopped for a red light at Yonge and Eglinton."

"What? Not an accident, I hope."

"Nothing like that," Ethan laughed. "I—what happened was—I realized I'm falling in love with you."

I was taken off guard. In the eight months we went out, Joey had never once said he loved me. "After just kissing?"

I asked stupidly, wishing I could see Ethan's face, knowing he was probably glad I couldn't.

He chuckled. "No, after you were such a good friend to me again today. Tina had no patience for Ellie and all her appointments and emergencies. It's so nice to spend time with someone who understands…and *then* there's the kissing."

"Lucy tried to talk to me about birth control tonight," I said.

"Why? Is she trying to get pregnant?" Ethan asked.

I cracked up. "Don't give her any ideas. Listen, Ethan—" I pressed my suddenly clammy hands on my pajama pants. "I have some pretty strong feelings for you, too."

"So…what are you wearing?" Ethan teased.

"Glad to see at least one of us hasn't lost our sense of humour. "

Ethan turned serious. "I wanted to also let you know we're definitely leaving for Ottawa in the morning, Tee. Ellie is much better. She's being transferred back to CHEO for another week of antibiotic treatment."

"So this is goodbye until Christmas?"

"Yeah. Once again, I'm going to miss you like crazy. So, where are we, Tee?"

"I've been wondering, too. Are we, like, *dating* now?"

Ethan paused so long I feared he'd say no, feared his bad experience with Tina had turned him off long-distance relationships despite our growing feelings for each other. Then I feared he'd say yes, feared my life was still too messed up to be a good girlfriend, feared sex would someday get in the way of our friendship. I feared it all might turn into a bitter mess like Aunt George's marriage to On-The-Road Stan. But then Ethan laughed and my fears went into dry dock. "Tee, 'just friends' don't kiss the way we did tonight. We're dating all right, whether we like it or not. And I think I like it."

I smiled into the phone, then yawned. "Me, too, but maybe you'll feel differently after I whip your butt on the fall exams."

"Keep dreaming, Sleepyhead."

# Part 4

*The first thing you must learn about canoeing is that the canoe is not a lifeless, inanimate object: it feels very much alive, alive with the life of the river…Anyone can handle a canoe in a quiet millpond, but in rapids a canoe is like a wild stallion. It must be kept on a tight reign. The canoeist must take the canoe where he or she wants it to go. Given the chance, the canoe will dump you overboard and continue down the river by itself.*

– Bill Mason

# Chapter 14

Mel and I, with an ecstatic Lucy in tow, arrived back at our North Creek bungalow two days before Christmas. For three weeks, contractors had been busy painting, delivering furniture, installing grab bars in the bathrooms and a ramp out back for Mel's wheelchair.

It was nice to be back in the house and town I grew up in—even with the changes, it felt like home. It was sad, too; Aunt George was so obviously missing from the otherwise familiar surroundings.

That very afternoon, Ethan called from the North Creek A&P and invited Ernie and me to dinner. His parents were going to the city to finish their Christmas shopping, leaving Ethan and Ellie at home to make do-it-yourself pizza. I knew Lucy wanted me to help her get the kitchen unpacked and organized, but Mel told me to go have a good time and insisted my share of the unpacking could wait. I thought of how many times Dr. Spellman had tried to impress the concept of compromise into our psyches, how despite my parents' efforts, old habits were dying hard. Would Lucy and Mel squabble over me forever or was it up to me to make the first move?

I didn't have much time to decide—Ethan and Wilma were right over. I'd offered to drive out to the farm later with the Jeep and save Ethan the trouble of driving me home, but Ethan insisted on picking me up, saying he'd explain after dinner. It ended up for the best. He saved the day *and* won my mother over forever when he volunteered to help Lucy and I fix up the kitchen before we left. The three of us worked like a well-oiled machine and had the whole miserable task done in less than an hour.

When Ethan and I finally escaped the bungalow, he gave me a hug that lifted me off the ground. Ernie danced around us excitedly, eager for his share of the affection.

"I've missed you, too," I laughed when he finally let me down.

"Even though I slaughtered you in Algebra?" Ethan grinned.

"*And* Chemistry."

Ethan laughed. "Not by much. And you did cream me in English and Biology."

"Face it, Ethan. We're a couple of overachievers."

As we approached Aunt George's property on our way to Cedar Bend, I asked Ethan to stop the truck. I'd been deathly afraid of how I'd react seeing the property for the first time since the fire, though Ethan assured me the rubble had been cleared out in preparation for the rebuilding, which would begin come spring. I got out of the truck, shut the passenger door, and leaned against it for the longest time, watching the late afternoon sun set over the birches and evergreens across the river. Despite the frigid December air, I didn't feel cold, just sad. The papers reported that the world had lost a talented, charismatic author, but *I'd* lost my good old Aunt George, my rock. My family was just Mel,

Lucy and I now, that ever-complicated love triangle. My eyes filled with tears.

I didn't hear Ethan come up beside me.

"Go ahead. Cry," he said, putting his arms around me and sheltering me from the wind.

"Come on," I said instead. I let Ernie out of the truck to roam and grabbed Ethan's hand. We quickly crunched across frozen dirt and old snow to the river. The channel was dark and choppy; despite the cold, it showed no signs of freezing solid anytime soon.

I kicked at some hard earth with the toe of my hiking boot until I dislodged a handful of small rocks.

Aunt George had a ritual. Whenever she was about to begin a new writing project, or make a major life decision, or just celebrate the changing of the seasons, she'd gather three rocks and toss them out into the river one at a time. The first rock was to commemorate the joys and lessons of the past. The second was to honour the adventure of the present. The third and final was to express hope for the future; it was the rock to wish on. Sometimes, Aunt George would stand on the riverbank for hours, reflecting, dreaming.

"What do you wish for?" Ethan asked after I tossed my third rock into the river. He gathered my cold hands in his.

I thought a minute, looking out over the water. "I used to have a clear map of where my life was heading; all smooth sailing on open waters. But now it's like I'm stuck in weeds, flailing off course. I've learned so much in these past six months, yet I feel so out of control, like I've lost my compass. Even my emotions used to be straightforward: happy, sad, angry, excited. Now, I have all these other feelings, toxic ones: grief, dread, anxiety, resentment. I get so scared that I'll never feel just plain old happy again." I looked up at Ethan. "I wished that sometime, sometime in the *next* six months, by graduation, I would find my way."

Ethan frowned. "Are all your new feelings toxic?"

I squeezed his hand. "No. There are these feelings I have for you."

Ethan's grinned. "Care to share?"

I sighed. "I don't know if I can. On the one hand, you're the best friend I've ever had—I don't want to jeopardize that. On the other hand..." I blushed.

Ethan nodded, but then his face fell. "You know, I still can't stop kicking myself for being such a jerk at Thanksgiving."

"Ethan?" I was a little exasperated. "Once and for all, you're forgiven. You've more than made amends. I'm no angel either—just ask Lucy. No question, meeting you was the best thing that happened to me this year."

The Stinson parents were just leaving the farm when Ethan and I arrived. After all that had happened between me and Ethan since September, it seemed strange that I'd never met them before. Mr. Stinson was a stocky, round-faced man with a hearty laugh and a strong Maritime accent; he pumped my hand enthusiastically. Ethan's mother had the most beautiful long black hair I'd even seen—she worked part-time at Hair Aware Salon in town. Her eyes twinkled when she took me aside and said, "Eleanor idolizes you like a big sister."

"Mom!" an embarrassed Ellie protested before taking off like a shot—with a hyped-up Ernie on her heels—to the fenced-in area out back. We knew Ernie would pee himself with happiness to see his brother Bert again, so the big family reunion was best held outdoors.

"And, Theresa," Mr. Stinson piped up. "I'm sure you're aware how Ethan feels about you." He guffawed and cuffed Ethan on the shoulder.

Ethan looked as though he wanted to crawl under the porch and die.

I smiled politely, glad that for once it was someone else's parents who were causing all the embarrassment.

Ethan called Ellie inside and led us to the kitchen where we pulled dough mix, sauce, meats, veggies, and four kinds of cheese from his grocery bags. Standing side by side at the counter, the three of us created personalized pizzas and sang along loudly with an old Christmas CD. While I tried to spread my pepperoni slices, green peppers, and mushrooms evenly, *logically*, over my amoeba-shaped crust, Ethan was busy rolling and moulding his dough into a fat Santa Claus character adorned with a sausage nose, olive eyes, onion-slice hair, and a tomato sauce suit.

"Ellie, who's that?" I asked. Her creation was decidedly feminine. Red pepper hair. Small mushroom ears. Long grated-carrot eyelashes. A sneering tomato slice mouth and down-turned green pepper eyebrows gave the pizza a personality, an attitude. Ethan was right: Ellie was an artist.

Ellie laughed so hard she had a coughing fit. "It's Tina's face when Bert started humping her leg!"

Dead silence. Ellie's face froze. She glanced over at Ethan, who shot her a look that could kill a cockroach. "Sorry," she mumbled to Ethan, then shrugged. "I thought you would have already told—"

"Ellie," Ethan interrupted, his voice ice. "Please bring in the dogs and play with them in your room. I'll call you when the pizza's ready."

Ellie slunk off. "Sorry," she mumbled again.

Ethan turned to me and sighed.

"Is she pregnant?" I asked, referring to Tina. Wasn't that always how it happened on TV—the guy moves on and the old girlfriend shows up at the door with "bad news"? Wasn't that pretty much how it happened with Mel and Lucy? When Mel got his Ph.D., he'd reluctantly left Lucy behind in Montreal and moved back to North Creek to start work at the college. Lucy came knocking two months later; her parents had thrown her out of the house when she informed them she'd dropped out of McGill and refused to have an abortion. According to Aunt George, Mel was the happiest man in the world that day—he still loved Lucy and was excited about becoming a father. They married at city hall two weeks later and the rest was misery. Sorry, I meant to say *history*.

"No!" Ethan was mortified.

"How do you know?" I asked.

"We only did it twice," he said sheepishly.

"How many times does it take in Newfoundland?"

Ethan smirked, his cheeks grew pink. "Tee, we were *careful*. Plus our last time together was in August. Wouldn't she be showing something if she were pregnant?"

"Was she wearing baggy clothes?"

"No. Just jeans and a turtleneck."

"Then I guess you're off *that* hook."

"Besides, she's been with…" Ethan's voice trailed off. He was still burned that Tina had cheated on him and made a mockery of their long-distance commitment. But he'd met my parents—living proof that, for better or worse, it's not over till it's over.

"So," I asked, "Tina was just in the neighbourhood?"

Ethan rolled his eyes. "Hardly. Tina's concert band won first place at the Newfoundland music festival and was invited to Ottawa for the Nationals. I had no warning; she just showed up at the door last Tuesday night and said the girl she was billeted with was waiting outside in the car. I don't even know how they managed to find the house."

"It's okay, Ethan. You don't have to explain."

But Ethan continued. "She and Doug broke up. He got an offer to play hockey for a college in the U.S. come January. He dumped her."

"So Tina wants to get back together with you?" I tried to sound nonchalant but—let's be serious—it mattered to me. A lot. Rich pizza aroma enveloped the kitchen, but I suddenly didn't feel hungry.

Ethan shrugged. "Yeah..." Long grim pause. "...But I told her no. Not a chance. No way. I told her I was seeing someone else. Then Bert, well, he started humping her leg."

I let out the deep breath I hadn't realized I was holding. "Too embarrassing. How come you got mad at Ellie for mentioning it to me?"

Ethan shrugged. "It wasn't that I didn't want you to know. I just wanted to forget the stupid night ever happened. Tina cried, ranted, hurled insults, made a big scene in front of my parents—who never liked her much to begin with. Under different circumstances, it might have been nice to see her again, just to say hi, catch up, but she made it so hard." He stared off into space. "Tina's not interested in being friends. Come to think of it we never *were* friends, not like you and me. With Tina, it was all about, well, the physical stuff. I told Tina I loved her, but I think I just loved messing around. We didn't have much in common; she wasn't what you'd call an intellectual. She liked that I'd do her math and biology homework; I liked that she was eager to tutor me in the practical aspects of sex ed." Ethan looked me in the eye. "With you, even though we haven't seen each other in *weeks*, it's like you're a vital piece in my jigsaw. There's been this 'connection' between us from day one, even when I still felt committed to Tina. We always have so much to talk about."

"And sex never crosses your mind?" I asked.

Ethan laughed. "Oh, at least a thousand times a day. But just talking about algebra with you gives me a hard-on."

After dinner, Ellie excused herself to call some friends and finish a Christmas wreath she was making for the front door.

"How's Ellie doing?" I asked Ethan when she'd disappeared up the stairs, the puppies at her heels. "She seems pretty energetic tonight."

Ethan shrugged. "Some days good, some days not. The tube is keeping her weight steady, but all that liquid being pumped in while she sleeps makes her wet the bed. The doctor says her body will get used to the extra fluids over time and the bedwetting will ease up, but she gets so embarrassed. She won't let anyone help her change the bed or do the laundry."

I was reminded of Mel when he first came out of the coma and couldn't do anything for himself. "What about Depends or something? She could put them on and take them off on her own. No one would have to know."

Ethan laughed. "My mom suggested that and Ellie took her head off. No way, she said, is she going to wear diapers like a baby. So instead, she's started setting her alarm at two-hour intervals. You should hear her, bumping the big pole with the suspended food bag along the hardwood floors four, five times a night. Mom suggested a bedpan, and again, Ellie took her head off. She's a proud, stubborn chick that sister of mine. No one's got the heart to tell her she's keeping the whole house awake at night."

"How are her lungs?" I couldn't help but notice that despite Ellie's high spirits that evening, her breathing seemed raspier than ever. A few times I'd even seen her hork huge green gobs into paper towels.

Ethan sighed. "The infections are getting more frequent and more severe. Used to be she'd get one to two bad ones a year; she'd go into the hospital for a course of I.V. antibiotics and come home good as new, at least for awhile. The antibiotics aren't really curing the infections anymore; they're just taking the edge off. You've seen her fingers, the way they bulb out? Ellie's self-conscious about them. She says they make her look like an extra-terrestrial."

"Why are they like that?"

"Lack of oxygen. There's not enough oxygen saturation in her blood to reach the extremities. Her toes are like that too," Ethan sighed. "Eventually she'll need supplemental oxygen just to breathe."

Ellie didn't deserve that shit in her life, no one did. "Ethan, didn't you mention that she might be eligible for a lung transplant? Wouldn't that help?"

"When and if she's deemed a candidate. The doctor's don't think she's sick enough yet to be on the list."

I hated the way he said "yet," like things would only get worse. My father's medical issues suddenly seemed minor by comparison. Mel had his share of troubles, but at least he could still take breathing for granted. For the first time, I really understood the magnitude of the stress Ellie, Ethan and their parents felt every day.

Ethan could read my mind. "You'd think I'd be used to it by now, but I just can't stand to see Ellie sick. She coughs so hard sometimes she throws up, or until, she says, her 'ribs rattle.' But coughing is good—bringing up the mucous is better than having it stay in her lungs and breed infections—but it's such a horrible, racking sound to come out of such a small body. I feel so helpless. I'd do anything to make it so she wouldn't have to go through this disease, but all I can do right now is rub her back and tell her jokes and treat her like a pesky little sister, because that's what she wants more than anything."

"What's that?" I asked.

Ethan sighed. "To feel normal."

"Maybe someday you really will find a cure, Ethan," I said hopefully.

He nodded. "But…well…it'll probably be too late for Ellie. She's too sick." Ethan's voice broke. "She's not going to be one of the ones who live to forty. I know it, she knows it, my parents know it, but no one talks about it."

"You seem to be doing a pretty good job of it, Ethan." Ellie was standing in the door frame. "I didn't mean to eavesdrop, but it's kind of hard not to when your own sorry life story is being poured out on the table. Ethan, I don't mind if she knows I'm dying, but did you have to mention the goddamn bedpan?"

I got up from the table and went to Ellie. "I'm sorry," I said to her. "It's my fault. I asked Ethan how you were doing. I was concerned about your breathing."

Ellie shrugged. "You could have just asked me yourself. It's pretty obvious I'm sick; CF is not a quiet disease, what with the coughing and wheezing and the motorized compressor and chest percussor. But whatever, Tee—I know your life's not a bed of roses, either." She quickly changed the subject. "Listen, can I see you a minute? In private? There's something I've been wanting to ask you. It'll only take a minute, then I'll disappear for the rest of the night. I know you and Ethan want time alone to suck face."

"Sure." I followed Ellie back up the stairs to her bedroom. She shooed Ernie and Bert out, closed the door behind us, and put a chair under the doorknob.

Ellie sat on her bed. "I have a strange request, but I have a reason. And don't go thinking I'm a lesbian—it's not that."

I laughed. "Okay."

"May I see your breasts?"

She was right, it was a strange request. But Ellie looked so serious, so concerned about something. "What the hey, we're all girls, right?" I pulled off my sweater and unhooked my bra.

Ellie scrutinized my chest silently for a long minute.

"Ellie is there something bothering you?"

She nodded, turned away, pulled off her own sweatshirt and tiny tank-style bra, and turned back to face me. She hid the tube protruding from her abdomen with her hand.

"Look at me!" she pouted, gesturing to her own small breasts. "I'm a *freak*. One is bigger than the other!"

I tried not to laugh. "Not by much. That's normal, Ellie. Besides, you're still growing."

Ellie looked dejected. "That's what Mom said, too, but what does she know? I needed to double-check."

"Glad I could help," I grinned.

Ellie raised a brow at my breasts. "You know, I think one of yours is a little bigger than the other, too."

"Yeah?" I turned towards the mirror. "Which one?"

Ellie laughed, a deep, raspy cackle. "Fooled you! Had you worried, though, didn't I? Now can I ask you a really embarrassing question?"

"Fire away," I said as we put our shirts back on.

"Do you let Ethan touch you...on your breasts?"

"Ellie...that's kind of private."

She blushed at my rebuke. "Let me rephrase. Hypothetical question: If a guy were to touch you on your breasts, how would he do it? Like, would he A: just make a grab at them directly, or B: kind of work his way across your stomach and up your ribs and then touch them?"

How did I get myself into these conversations? "B is the preferred approach. Ellie has some guy at school been putting the moves on you?"

She shook her head. "No. But there's a boy that likes me. And I kind of like him. He kissed me after the Holiday Dance last week, just on the cheek. But what if someday he or some other guy tries to touch my lopsided breasts and reaches under my shirt and feels my tube instead? What if he is so grossed out he pukes?"

The kid has a fatal disease and this is what she worries about? "Ellie," I said. "Any guy who would be grossed out or turned off by your tube has no business putting his hand inside your shirt anyway. Does this guy from school, the one who kissed you, does he know about your G-tube?"

Ellie nodded. "All the kids in my class know about it; they knew I was going to Toronto for surgery. But I don't go around showing it to people. My days of wearing cropped tops are over."

I thought about it. "Maybe it would help if you didn't try to hide it so much. If you act comfortable with it, like it's no big deal, then other people will too, eventually. There's a girl in my homeroom, Kellie, who was in a bad skiing accident and has a prosthetic leg. She wears shorts and skirts and whatever she wants, and people are so used to seeing it they hardly notice it now."

"Does she have a boyfriend?"

I nodded. "Cute guy, too."

Ellie pondered. "So you think I should stop changing in the bathroom before gym class? Just...let it all hang out?"

"Yeah." I nodded. "Try it. Some kids will stare or ask too many questions, and some might even say mean stuff, but your friends will be there for you."

Ellie looked relieved. "That's what this girl Barbara from the CHEO clinic said, too. She's had a G-tube for three years."

"May I see your tube?" I asked.

"I guess." Ellie lifted her shirt, exposing the short rubber tube. "See, the balloon that holds it in place is inflated with water through this small valve. And the Ensure liquid goes through this bigger valve." Ellie unscrewed the bigger valve; air escaped making a gurgling sound. "It needs to be burped sometimes," Ellie laughed. "Ethan said the next time I get on his case, he'll screw his bicycle pump onto the food valve and blow me up."

"Nice brother."

"You like him a lot, eh?"

"Yeah, a lot."

Ethan looked perplexed when I rejoined him in the kitchen; I'd been with Ellie a good half-hour. "I thought you'd be in there all night. What were you talking about?"

I shook my head. "Top secret girl-stuff."

"Spare me the gruesome details. Grab your coat. I want to show you something in the barn. It's a surprise. Here," he said, picking my scarf off the chair. "Let me tie this around your eyes."

Ethan led me down an icy gravel path to the barn. I tripped over a rock at one point and we both landed in a hard snow pile. We stayed on the ground for a good ten minutes wrestling, laughing, trying to shovel ice down each other's backs. Somewhere in the tussle, my blindfold fell off. Ethan tied it back on and helped me to my feet.

"Okay, take a deep breath," Ethan said once I'd been led through the side barn door. I did, and my nose was assaulted with the smell of wet hay and old manure. I was about comment on the florid aroma when Ethan pulled the scarf from around my eyes. *"Ta-da!"*

I couldn't speak.

Ethan was too excited to notice. "I worked on it in Mr. Harnett's garage every weeknight for the past month or so. He dropped it off here yesterday before he and his family left for their Florida vacation. I know it won't fit down your chimney, but it slides right onto my truck bed. We can sneak it into your garage when I drop you off later tonight. Is that okay?" Ethan paused. "Well, do you like it?"

"Ethan, it's the most beautiful thing I've even seen," I whispered, still overcome. "You finished it all yourself?"

Ethan nodded. "Mostly. Mr. Harnett fed me dinner and kept me company lots of nights."

I'd forgotten all about the canoe. So much had happened.

I finally found my voice. "Thank you so much!" I jumped up and down, threw my arms around Ethan's neck and held on for dear life. I was laughing and crying. This guy really did love me.

"You're strangling me!" Ethan pried me off him long enough to catch his breath. "No thanks required. It was a lot of fun. And your dad deserves credit for most of the work, Tee. I just finished her off."

The *ping, ping, ping* was so intense at that moment, I felt like a pinball wizard, like I'd just won a slots jackpot in Vegas. "Mel will be so surprised!" I wrapped my arms around Ethan again, more gently this time. "I love you, Ethan. You know that, right?"

He grinned. "I'd hoped."

For the first time in what felt like ages, I wasn't fighting a raging current of mixed-up emotions. I hadn't forgotten the turbulence of the past, and I knew not what rocks and rapids lay ahead, but for then, at least when it came to Ethan, I felt ready to go with the flow. And it felt wonderful.

# Chapter 15

Christmas Eve morning was sombre. For the past three years, it had been Aunt George's day: she'd have me and Mel over for dinner, I'd help her decorate cookies, we'd trim a tree, and then we'd all bundle up and head out to the candlelight service at North Creek United, where Aunt George sang in the choir. Christmas Day she always spent in the city, at a shelter, serving dinner to a hundred women in crisis and their children. It was Lucy's idea for us to honour Aunt George's tradition this year, and the shelter readily accepted our offer of help. Lucy would assist in the kitchen. I'd serve. Mel volunteered to be Santa and hand out gifts donated by the Christmas Wish Foundation—he already had the red suit and extra padding laid out in the spare bedroom.

But around noon that Christmas Eve, Mel became agitated. He'd started taking pills to prevent muscle spasms in his hands when he worked at his new computer for extended periods. And they worked. But since Mel had started taking them, his moods had been unpredictable—one minute he'd be cheerful and chatty; the next he'd be edgy, restless, and more easily frustrated than usual at his limitations. Mel suspected all along it was the pills and told the doctor he hadn't felt "right" since he'd started taking them, but his neurologist, full of that doc-speak bullshit I despised so much, told Mel to, you guessed it, "give it time."

By mid-afternoon, Lucy suggested Mel go take a nap. He'd been pacing the floor for over an hour—clomp-step, clomp-step with the cane, wearing treads in the new carpet.

"I'm not tired," he sneered, going over to the window. "It's mild outside today. I'll go for a walk around the block."

"Want me to go with you?" I asked, thinking he might like the company.

Mel snapped. "I'm not a goddamned baby! I think I can make it around the block without a nursemaid."

I was too stunned to retort. My face flushed as if he'd slapped me.

"Mel, I don't think that's what she meant," Lucy put in her two cents. It was weird, Lucy defending me against Mel.

But Mel turned on her, too. "Can't a man have five *fucking* minutes to himself?"

Lucy froze. That's it, I thought. She'll be packed up and back in Toronto before the end of the week. Who could blame her? Who'd look after Mel then? Could I do it alone? I hated to admit it, even to myself, but Lucy had been the glue holding things together these past two months.

Clomp-step, clomp-step—Mel struggled with his coat. Clomp-step, clomp-step—he was out the front door, cursing at the steps as he made his way down, hanging onto the iron railing for dear life.

Lucy moved behind me where I was watching Mel out the window. Despite my anger, I was praying he wouldn't fall.

She laid a hand on my back. "He'll be okay later," she said. "You know how these moods run in cycles. Once he gets the meds changed—"

"We won't be able to volunteer at the shelter tomorrow," I interrupted. "We can't take the chance of him cursing and pacing the floors like a crazy man. Those women and children go to the shelter to get away from all that."

Lucy nodded. "Good point," she said and went to make the call to cancel.

When Mel wasn't back an hour later, I wondered out loud if I should go out looking for him. Maybe he'd slipped on a patch of ice and couldn't get up.

Lucy shook her head. "No. Give him a while longer. He's probably chatting with Frank Miller down the street. Someone would call if Mel was in trouble; the whole town knows him."

"You're right," I said, but kept my eyes trained on the front window anyway.

"Aren't you seeing Ethan today?" Lucy asked a while later. Watching me stress out about Mel was stressing her out.

I shook my head. "He's doing family stuff today. He's going to stop by tomorrow."

Lucy nodded. "You came home pretty late last night. I heard you tiptoeing in the hall. I know we decided you don't need a curfew, but—"

As long as she didn't hear Ethan and me in the garage. He and I had snuck the canoe into the garage a little after one a.m. Covered with an old plastic tarp, it blended with the other stuff out there: several cords of wood, old furniture Lucy intended to put at the curb on garbage day, stacks of plywood and two by fours left behind by the contractors who built the wheelchair ramp out back. I doubted Mel would take notice. "Yeah, I'm sorry," I said. "I should have called. Ethan and I just got talking and whatever." And whatever—there was an understatement.

"Mom?" I asked a few minutes later. I wasn't sure she could help me, but I wanted to know what love was supposed to feel like—not physically—but inside your head. Was love supposed to clarify things in your mind or was it doomed to confuse you, make you second-guess your decisions, give you nightmares?

"Mmm?"

"I've been thinking about the offer from B.C.—"

"Theresa! Lucy! *Get your asses out here!*" Mel screamed from the back porch.

"Dear God, what now?" Lucy sighed.

"Oh, no," I sucked in my breath.

"What?"

"He's been in the garage."

"So?" Lucy asked, but I was already flying out the door.

Even in the dark garage, filled with dust and tension thick as a McDonald's shake, the uncovered cedar-strip canoe shone like a star. It was such a fine piece of work, representing over a thousand of Mel's hard-earned bucks and two-years worth of his labour. It was the materialization of a dream, his dream.

"What the hell is this?" Mel waved his cane at the canoe, scowling.

"It's your Christmas surprise, Dad," I whispered, feeling sucker-punched.

"It's a goddamn surprise all right! I told you to get rid of it!"

I took a deep breath. "Dad, it seemed a shame not to finish it. It was one of the few things of value that survived the fire at Aunt George's."

Mel glared at me. "Well, who the hell finished it? I know it wasn't you."

"Ethan did."

"Ethan?" Mel asked, confused.

"Yeah, Ethan. He worked on it in Mr. Harnett's garage."

A blue vein bulged on Mel's forehead. "Ron knew about this?"

I nodded.

Mel yelled, "I can't use a canoe now, Theresa! You must

know that. What were you thinking!"

My eyes burned, but I wouldn't back down. It was the bad medication making Mel irrational, I kept telling myself. "I was thinking we could still go on our trip this spring. I can do most of the paddling, or maybe we could rig up a small motor, or—"

Mel interrupted. "Have you thought about how I'm supposed to get in and out of a canoe? How I'm supposed to hobble around a campground on this cane? Just *fucking* get rid of it!" He hurled the cane at the canoe, missing it by a good four feet. *"I never want to see it again!"*

"Calm down, Mel." Lucy stepped between Mel and I, like a tiny lioness preparing to defend her oversized cub.

"Shut up, Lucy. I'm talking to my daughter."

Lucy spat back, "She's my daughter, too! We're going inside, Mel. You're making a scene." She took Mel's arm with the intention of leading him into the house.

"Just stay out of it, Lucy!" Mel shrugged her off and pushed her away. Lucy stumbled.

I lost it, or perhaps, for the first time in my life, I *found* it—the compassion and understanding to stick up for my mother when she was being bullied. "Don't you touch her, Mel!" I screamed in his face.

Before Lucy or I could see it coming, Mel raised his right arm, his good arm, and with all the strength he could muster, punched me right in the mouth.

I took off, ran to my room, left behind a trail of blood on the expensive hall carpet. I slammed the door and locked it.

Through the wall, I heard Lucy in the kitchen on the phone. In a shaky voice she requested an ambulance.

I peered out my bedroom window. Mel was banging on the back door, yelling for someone to let him in. Lucy wasn't answering; I realized she'd locked him out. Thankfully most of our nearest neighbours had left town for the holidays. *Look at the crazy Stanfords*, they'd whisper amongst themselves. We'd been back in North Creek less than forty-eight hours and things were already falling to pieces.

When she got off the phone, Lucy padded down the hall and knocked softly but insistently on my bedroom door. "Theresa, let me in. I need to see your face."

"I'm okay," I murmured, not opening the door. "I'll clean the rug. I just need a minute to myself."

"Forget the rug; just open the door. *Please.*" Lucy was pleading now.

I winced at the sight of my face in the mirror over the dresser. The setting on Mel's alumni ring had torn my lip, but I doubted it was deep enough to require stitches. My teeth ached, but I'd wiggled them all and none were loose. My jaw was swelling to the size of a grapefruit, but I could still open and close it. If Mel had been stronger, he might have knocked my teeth clear out the back of my head, such had been his fury.

"I'm okay," I repeated. "I don't need to go to the hospital."

Lucy sounded on the verge of tears. "I called the ambulance for Mel, honey. He's having a bad reaction to his medication. We should have demanded that arrogant Toronto neurologist do something right away. I'm going to insist they take Mel into the city. I don't know how long we'll be; it's a holiday, so the hospital might be short-staffed. I need to see you before we go to make sure you're okay."

Lucy wasn't going to take no for an answer and I didn't want her trying to break the door down; I'd seen enough violence for one day. So I wiped the blood still oozing from my mouth onto my sleeve and opened the door.

"Oh, dear God, what did he do?" Lucy started to cry for real. Hard, racking sobs. "Come with us, Theresa. You need to get checked out."

"No, Lucy, I'm okay. I've had worse fat lips from playing road hockey," I lied. "I'll put some frozen peas on it, okay? I know Mel's crazy right now, that he didn't mean to hurt me. But if I go with you, they'll bring in that stupid social worker again and accuse Mel of being a child abuser." I heard ambulance sirens growing closer. Mel was still pounding away at the door. "You better go." I was firm.

"Theresa, are you sure you won't come?"

I nodded my head.

"Then please, call my cell if you need me."

"Okay." Just go, I thought. Just go, already. Leave me alone with my fat lip and my misery.

"Oh, and Theresa?" Lucy turned back.

"Yeah?"

"I know you meant well, but maybe Ethan or someone could come and take the canoe away. Or there's that camp up near Port Elmsley. Maybe we could donate it. It really is a beautiful canoe."

"That's Merrywood Camp, Lucy. It's a camp for kids with physical disabilities. Cerebral Palsy, Muscular Dystrophy, *head injuries*."

"I know, Theresa, but I've seen them out in canoes on the lake when I've driven by in the summer."

Duh. "That's my point, Lucy. Mel doesn't have to give up his canoe."

"I know, honey. But Mel doesn't *want* it anymore. He has a new life now. New dreams. New plans."

I wanted a new life, too.

"The canoe will be gone by the end of the day," I said, my voice hard. I slowly shut the bedroom door in Lucy's face.

# Chapter 16

For an hour I lay on my bed. With frozen peas on my jaw and hot tears on my cheeks, I tried to figure out what I was going to do about my screwed up life. When I failed to find any answers on the bedroom ceiling, I ran through algebra problems in my head until I fell asleep.

Just after the sun set, I woke up, my mind strangely clear. I stole out the back door to the garage and gathered all the rope I could find. Struggling under its weight, I angled one end of the canoe onto the Jeep's roof rack, then hoisted the rest up and secured it with rope. I tossed my knapsack and the beavertail paddle Ethan had hand-made over several long lunch hours in the wood shop into the back seat, then set out along the back roads with no clear destination in mind. I didn't want to head through downtown and run the risk of being seen by someone I knew. Thankfully Mr. Harnett was in Florida until New Year's Eve; were he to see me, I'd be off to the county hospital come hell or high water. He might be Mel's best friend, but he was also my teacher. I'd have to find a way to avoid Ethan, too, for the week or so it would take the bruises to fade. It would be a lonely week; if I craved anything right then it was Ethan's arms around me.

It was Christmas Eve and I was alone, more alone than

I'd ever felt in my life. I missed Aunt George so much. Despite her ties to my father, she would have been mad as hell about what he'd done to me. She would've held me in her big embrace and made me tomato soup and dispensed her no-nonsense advice. She'd know what—if anything— could be saved of the dreams and plans I'd made before Mel's injury.

Without ever intending to, I pulled the Jeep into the drive of Aunt George's property and took a short moonlit walk down to the river, retracing the bootprints Ethan and I had left the day before. I thought of the rocks we'd tossed in the river, of the wishes I'd made for the future. Anger coursed through my veins. I knew I'd never make any headway caught as I was in the tangles of my parents' new relationship and my father's rocky rehabilitation.

All along, I'd committed myself to seeing Mel through his recovery. Now I felt guilty for resenting the disruption to my life, for wanting out. But at the same time, hadn't Mel been pushing me away—first by leaving me out of the loop as he and Lucy planned their new life together, now by refusing my efforts to salvage our canoe trip? I didn't want to run away from him, but I felt I no longer belonged. I still loved my parents, but I hated myself when I was with them. Give it time, Dr. Spellman would say. But time was running out. Meds, or no meds, I wasn't going to let Mel hurt me again.

"Aunt George," I called to the stars overhead, my eyes blurred with fresh tears. *"What should I do?"*

The night was silent but for the comforting and familiar rhythm of the river.

"Do what's in your heart," she replied.

I figured Aunt George's property was as good a place as any to stash the canoe until I could find a good home for it. If it hadn't been for Ethan's hard work, I'd have just torched the damn thing and been done with it.

The moon was bright overhead. The absence of wind gave the river the illusion of calm. Although a thin crust of ice had developed along the riverbank, the channel was still open. Definitely navigable. I decided to take the canoe out—for just a few minutes. So I could tell Ethan I gave it a test drive.

I untied the canoe. Dragged it across snow and mud from the Jeep to the river. Then I went back for the paddle on the back seat. I had no life vest, but I wouldn't be going far. Just a quick trip to the bend and back. Less than a kilometre. I zipped my Gore-Tex jacket tight, pulled the hood up over my ears, and slipped on my leather gloves. All set.

I took a deep breath, pushed off the dock, and broke easily through the thin ice near the shore into the channel. In the far distance I could hear bells ringing out Christmas carols. *Silent Night. Joy To The World.* I hummed along. Smiled at the irony.

I kept a steady J-stroke. I reached the bend and kept going, so lost in thought that I failed to notice the change in the wind or the clouds that obscured the moonlight. The dark and the quiet, once soothing, grew spooky.

*BANG!*

"What was that!" I yelled out into the night. Straining my eyes to regain my bearings, I realized I'd drifted off course towards the shallow rock-and-ice-strewn riverbank.

I had trouble turning the canoe back towards Aunt George's. I was a fair canoeist, had soloed at summer camp on flat water during daylight, but I was no expert when it came to paddling at night on a fast-flowing river in the dead of winter. The wind had picked up considerably. The temperature was dropping. I grasped too late that I'd been paddling with, not against, the current. I'd have to pull like hell to make it back. For the first time since setting out, I realized I'd been reckless.

*BANG!*

I hit another rock. The canoe whipped around in the strong wind. Pellets of snow began an insistent drum roll on my hood. I knew the wind and the current would soon overcome my quickly diminishing arm strength.

Calm down, I told myself. What were my options? I could try to make it back around the bend, I thought. Find a place to dock the canoe on the riverbank and hike back to Aunt George's. But the channel was wider now, the current more turbulent. Even if I managed to turn the canoe back, my strongest strokes would make no headway. I was no match for Mother Nature, who seemed more than a little pissed off at me.

*BANG!*

My paddle dropped from my numb fingers into the water and was swept away before I could reclaim it. The calm river I'd ventured out on had become like something out of *The River Wild*. The fun, if that's what I'd been having, was over. Option two: I could curl into a ball, close my eyes, and let the current carry me to the steep rapids a few kilometres downstream. In other words, I could let myself die. The thought didn't scare me, I realized, but it would look like I'd *planned* to commit suicide, and I hadn't, at least not on any conscious level.

I did have third option. Ethan's farm was only another kilometre or so downstream. There was no way I'd be able to guide the canoe to the riverbank without a paddle, but if I bailed a little before I reached the Stinson property, I could maybe swim to shore. If I didn't die of hypothermia first.

I had no idea what time it was. I prayed the Stinson's had their lights on so I'd be able to locate their house in the darkness. I prayed they hadn't gone to church in town. If I showed up at their door only to find no one home, I'd surely freeze on the spot.

There it was! The Stinson farmhouse was up ahead on the left beyond a stand of maples. I recognized the round window on the second floor landing and the red and white Christmas lights along the side porch. I had no time to second guess whether my plan was viable; the canoe was out of control now, rocking side to side, spinning in circles, being hurried along by the violent wind and current.

It was time to jump ship. With stiff fingers, I unlaced my heavy hiking boots and tossed them overboard. I said good-bye to the canoe and apologized for not treating it with more respect. I said a prayer and hit the icy river with a grand splash that sent me underwater. I surfaced, gasping, taking in water through my nose. Sputtering, I caught my breath, swallowed the urge to panic. Though my ski jacket provided me with some insulation, it weighed me down and slowed my strokes as I fought the current and struggled to keep my bearings. From the water, the light in the Stinson's window was obscured by trees; I could see nothing ahead but the dark outline of the maples. As I grew closer to shore, I was forced to punch through quarter-inch ice with each stroke. I don't know what gave me the strength to keep going.

I felt only minor relief when I crawled out of the water and up the slippery bank to dry land. My hands, feet and face were numb, and my limbs were heavy with exhaustion. I was blinded by darkness. As I lay there, the urge to nap was overwhelming. Sleepily, I reached up and felt my wet hair; already it was freezing stiff. I knew I needed to move. If I made it through the forest it was only another hundred feet to the house. I took a deep breath and pulled myself up using a maple trunk for support. Raising my hands to shelter my face from branches and other obstacles invisible in the dark, I crept low in my sock feet through the trees, keeping the sound of the river at my back to avoid travelling in circles.

Three minutes later, the trees thinned and Ethan's house came into view once again.

# Part 5

*Love many, trust few, and always paddle your own canoe.*

– Bumper sticker

# Chapter 17

Ethan took one look out the kitchen window and threw open the screen door. "Tee! What happened to you?"

"Long story." My teeth were chattering, my nose was running, my hair was stringy and stiff. I'd all but forgotten my cut lip and swollen jaw.

"Well, come inside!" Ethan dragged me dripping up the stairs to his bedroom. Quickly, he pulled sweatpants, a T-shirt, and a thick, long-sleeved pullover from the closet. He rummaged quickly in his dresser and tossed a pair of wool socks and long underwear to the pile.

"Get out of that wet stuff!" He made a mad dash down to the kitchen and returned seconds later with a stack of towels still warm from the dryer.

My toes and ears stung as I thawed. Ethan looked away while I pried my clothes off, not that I cared at that point about whether he saw me naked, or about anything else, for that matter. My fingers were so numb I needed his help with my shirt buttons.

When I was re-dressed in his big, warm boy-clothes, Ethan led me back to the kitchen and pulled out a chair. He wrapped a blanket around my shoulders and nuked me a jumbo mug of hot chocolate.

He waited silently for me to take a few sips of the hot, sweet liquid. The heat stung my swollen mouth, but I was grateful for the fluid warmth that began to radiate through my extremities. I was lucky to have eluded severe frostbite.

Finally Ethan said, "So spill it, Tee. I'm serious. What the hell happened to you?"

I shrugged. "I took a swim in the river."

He was livid. "This is no time for your smart-ass comments! Tell me what happened."

So I did, all of it. How Mel had flown into a psychotic rage when he'd seen the canoe. How I'd driven to Aunt George's and had gone a little crazy myself. How the canoe was gone now, most likely smashed to smithereens below the rapids.

Ethan came around behind my chair and rubbed my aching shoulders through the blanket. "Tee, promise me you'll never do anything like that again, never take chances out on the water. My parents *drowned*, Tee. Please promise me you'll never take chances like that again. Promise me." His voice was a dark blend of anger and fear.

I turned my head towards him, taking his warm hands in my cold ones. "I'm so sorry, Ethan."

*"Promise me!"*

"I promise." I meant it, too. Ethan had made good on his vow to stay sober; the least I could do was stay off the river after dark. I took a deep breath. "I'm sorry, too, about the canoe. All your hard work. All those hours wasted."

"They weren't wasted, Tee. I didn't finish the canoe for Mel; I finished it for you. The look on your face when you saw it Tee, I can't explain it. It's like you...sparkled. For the first time since I've met you, you seemed truly happy. That made every hour I spent on the canoe worth it for me. And no one can take that moment away. From either of us."

"You should have taken a picture, because you're unlikely to see that happy, sparkly face again anytime soon."

Ethan gave me a long, appraising look. "Tee, are you sure you don't want to see a doctor? Your face is a mess. You're still shivering. I'll come with you, stay with you."

I shook my head. "I'll be okay."

Ethan didn't answer; he started rubbing my shoulders again.

Then it hit me. Ethan was alone. We were alone.

I turned in the chair again. "Ethan, why are you alone? Where is your family? It's Christmas Eve. My family is insane, but you should be with your family wherever they are, not home alone with a crazy girl who just did the Polar Bear plunge. You—"

"Whoa, buddy," Ethan said. He let go of my shoulders, led me over to the couch in the family room, sat down with me, and held my cold hands. "Ellie's at the hospital. Mom and Dad brought her in to CHEO this afternoon. I would've gone with them, but my boss at the farm called and asked if I could take a quick run over to fix some fences that blew down on the east perimeter. It's a holiday, so they offered to pay double. Call me an opportunist, but—"

"But Ellie? Will she be okay? Is it her lungs? Did something go wrong with the tube?" I couldn't believe Ethan didn't seem more concerned.

Ethan shook his head and laughed. "It's not the CF this time. Ellie was practicing some funky dance moves in her room, jumping on the bed like she's been told not to do a million times. She lost her balance, fell off onto the floor, and broke her wrist. No big deal."

I knew there were people who might consider it callous to make light of a broken wrist. But Ethan and I both knew that on the long continuum of bad things that can happen to the human body, a broken wrist was, indeed, small potatoes.

"When will they be back?"

Ethan shrugged. "I don't know. With all the walk-in clinics closed early today, the emergency ward is hopping. Dad called about an hour ago frustrated that Ellie still hadn't been sent for X-rays. They should have just taken her to the county hospital instead of making a trip to the city. My parent's aren't used to long emergency room waits. They get faster service when Ellie's gasping for air and coughing up blood."

I was shocked. "Ellie does that? Cough up blood?"

Ethan nodded. "Yeah. Sometimes the lung infections erode a capillary. She felt a bleed one time during a school concert, said it didn't hurt, just felt like a worm crawling in her chest. She never said a word to anyone until the show was over."

"Wouldn't blood in her lungs make her cough?"

"Ellie can suppress her cough when she feels she needs to, if she's at church or the movies. It's not good for her to do that—it's best to bring up as much mucous as possible—but she gets embarrassed when her coughing draws attention from people. And during a bleed, coughing can make it worse."

I sighed. "She really can't win, can she."

"She's a pretty good sport about it, all things considered."

"Doesn't she get angry sometimes?" There I was at Ethan's, bitching about my own sorry life again, when Ellie struggled every day just to breathe.

"Sure," Ethan said. "She gets furious. And she's got that just-turned-thirteen hormone thing going on, too. She yells, cries, stomps her feet at the slightest provocation, usually me, but it's been worse lately. Two weeks ago at an appointment, she found out her friend Marcie, one of the clinic regulars, had died. She was only fifteen. Ellie didn't want to talk about it with anyone. She pretended she didn't care, but as soon as she came home she went to her room, slammed the door and threw things at the wall for over an hour. But then she came out, did her mask treatment, took her pills and kept going. She's been living with CF her whole life. She usually accepts it.

So you have an easier time accepting it, Ethan, I thought. She's protecting you. She loves you and doesn't want you to worry any more than you have to.

"Mel's not there yet, in terms of accepting his condition," I said. "The hundred per cent recovery came up short."

Ethan's voice was gentle. "Tee, is it Mel who hasn't accepted it, or you?"

I sighed. "I guess I *was* pretty stupid for thinking that if the canoe was finished Mel would keep our trip plans. But lots of disabled people canoe, and—"

Ethan interrupted. "*Stupid?* No way. Of course your father could still go canoeing. But think about what that canoe represented to him: the beauty of what he could create with his hands, the power of what he could propel with his own strength. Didn't you say he'd planned the trip so he could lead you down the river he'd explored as a boy, show you the secret coves and back trails? Maybe he thinks it wouldn't be the same now."

I knew he was right. Besides the paddle, the canoe, and my boots, I lost other things out on the river that night: some myths of my childhood, some outdated hopes and dreams, the fear of being swept away by a restless current. And I found some things too: independence, courage, and the knowledge that it was entirely up to me to decide the course of my future. Here seemed like a good place to start.

"Ethan?" I took a deep breath, held his hand tight. "I realized tonight that it's time for me to find my own river, explore my own back trails." I paused and took another breath. "I'm leaving."

"Don't go yet," Ethan said, misunderstanding. He jumped up from the couch. "I'll drive you home or back to the Jeep if you really have to go now, but I'd like if you could stay. Are you hungry? There's a ton of food in the refrigerator: fish, potatoes, apple pie—stuff that's not hard to chew. We can—"

*Do what's in your heart*, Aunt George had told me time and again.

I stood up and wrapped my arms around him. "I'm not leaving *you*, Ethan. I'm leaving town. I'm going to accept the early-admission offer from B.C. I leave in a week."

Ethan was silent for a long minute. He stiffened in my arms and I let go. He was confused, hurt, and more than a little angry. "When did you decide?"

"When I was out on the river. You're the first person I've told."

"Should I feel *honoured*?" he sneered.

Tears sprung to my eyes. "I hoped you might feel happy for me."

Ethan rolled his eyes. "You only arrived back in North Creek yesterday. What about *us*, Tee? And what was last night in the barn? A thank-you bonus for finishing the canoe? I don't need to be one of the goddamn Blue Jays to know when I've made it to third base."

My first impulse was to slap Ethan's sorry face, but instead I slumped back onto the couch, closed my eyes, and tried to hold back the bile that was scorching my throat.

I looked up a few minutes later and through blurry eyes saw Ethan sitting at the kitchen table, his head in his hands. He looked up, too, came back over to the couch, and sat down. "I'm sorry, Tee. That was uncalled for." His voice broke.

"Damn right it was."

He took my hand. "Tee, I'd understand it if you had to go for family reasons, like when you went to Toronto, or when I had to leave Newfoundland. But…I love you, Tee. I just…I thought we had something special."

"We do. Or we *did*, until that comment about the barn."

"Tee, I'm sorry. You caught me off guard. I just said the first nasty thing that came to mind."

"You know last night wasn't about thanks. You *know* that, Ethan."

"What was it about?"

"For me? Wanting to be close to you? I love you, too, you jerk."

"Then why are you leaving again so soon? Just answer me that."

I thought maybe I should just borrow some shoes and go. I didn't know how to explain to Ethan what I was still grasping to understand myself.

Ethan could sense my frustration. His voice softened. "Tee, please tell me what's going on inside you."

I sucked in my breath, let it out slowly. "Earlier you said that last night when I saw the canoe was the first time you'd seen me truly happy."

"You weren't happy?"

"No, I *was* happy. Deliriously happy. And I realized that knowing you, being with you makes me happy. And God knows I haven't had many opportunities to be happy lately. I left you last night thinking I'd do just about anything for you. Give you a kidney. Lay down in front of a train. Swing naked from the chandelier. Anything. I couldn't sleep. I was convinced I was going to try for late admission to Queen's, study East Coast history, strive to become a future-geneticist's wife. I had our carpool schedule all worked out. I had names for our first two children picked out. *And it scared the crap out of me.* I realized that the only other person that had that kind of hold on me was *my father*. Don't get me wrong, there was never anything sick or incestuous about me and Mel, but I was so busy pleasing him all the time that I had no time to figure out what I wanted for myself. When I was ten, he coached hockey, so I played hockey, even though I wasn't very good at it. When I was fourteen, he took up running and I joined the cross-country team. I'm not like you, Ethan; I'm not gifted at science and math. I work my *ass* off to make the grades I do. And I did it all for Mel, because he wants me to be a zoologist."

"But you want to be a zoologist, too, don't you?"

"Sure I do. I really do. But I've never considered being anything else."

"So what does this have to do with you and me?"

"I love Mel, always will, but I don't love who I've become. This confused kid still trying to please her father, but not knowing what he wants anymore. All I have to show for it is a fat lip. And I love you, Ethan. I came out of the river tonight vowing to make a new life for myself and the first thing I did was show up on your doorstep—that says something. But until last night, you'd only known the tragic Tee with the messed-up parents who cried at the drop of a hat.

"That happy girl you met in your barn last night, the Tee who wasn't afraid of her feelings, who was willing to…to explore new ones with you, is the me I want to be more often. But to do that I have to figure out who I am and what I want for myself, by myself. I need to figure out how to love my parents and love you and not lose myself in the bargain. I don't want to start resenting you the way I've started resenting my father.

"So you want to break up?"

I took another deep breath and shook my head. "Ethan, you asked what last night was. For me, it was a commitment. To you, to us. Then tonight, just before I jumped out of the canoe, I made a commitment to myself. To give B.C. and Zoology and independence my best shot. One commitment doesn't have to negate the other."

"And do I have any say in this relationship?"

I nodded. "You have all the say now—I've said my piece. I know your last long-distance experience didn't work, so if you want to quit now, I'll be sad, but I'll understand."

Ethan took a long time to reply. "I'm not a quitter, but will I ever see you? B.C. is so far away. I have to save for university. I can't just—" One thing I would have to be sensitive of was the fact that Ethan, while not dirt poor, didn't have a lot of money for extras, like frequent plane trips to Vancouver. But I was, through no fault of my own, a rich girl now.

I cut Ethan off, smiling for the first time in over an hour. "Aunt George's zillion Air Miles and frequent flyer points were transferable. She'd been saving them for me all along, knowing I'd be finished high school some day and could use them for university commutes or a trip to Europe or whatever. But if I transfer them to you, you'll be able to visit as often as you like. She'd want you to have them; she had high hopes for you and me. Consider it a Christmas gift."

Ethan looked concerned. "That's really generous, Tee, but what will *you* use when you need to travel?"

I figured he should be let in on some simple facts. "Ethan, my dad got most of Aunt George's money, and some went to charity and some was set aside for the building and maintenance of the writer's colony on her property. But I got some, too. I'm not a zillionaire, not by a long shot, but I'll get back here often; there's the wedding in February, graduation in June—I wouldn't miss your speech for the world—and I'll—"

Ethan interrupted. "You don't know I'll be valedictorian for sure. You still have a chance."

"Not unless you actually *flunk* next semester."

"Want me to?"

"Don't you dare."

"—and I'll have a month off in August when my summer classes end," I continued. "And when we're not together there's e-mail and—"

"Cyber-sex?" Ethan grinned, warming to the idea.

"There's just one other thing," I said.

"What's that?"

"No games. If you find it's not working for you, if you meet someone else, or just don't want to continue, then don't stress over it or try to keep it going if you know it's not what you want anymore. Just tell me it's time to let go. Maybe then we can still be friends, because as long as our parents still live in the same town, chances are we'll run into each other from time to time."

Ethan nodded. "And you'll do the same for me?"

I gave him a three-finger salute. "Scout's honour."

We sat on the couch for a long while, not knowing what else to say. All the talking had made my swollen mouth ache; I'd been trying too hard not to lisp or slur. For the first time I understood how hard it must have been for Mel to talk for long periods. I felt bad for all the times I'd chatted him up when he probably just wanted to read or relax but was too proud to say so.

Ethan kissed my cheek, went to the kitchen, and returned with a bottle of Tylenol, antiseptic wipes, a tube of

Polysporin, and a bag of frozen corn.

"Do I look like a prizefighter?" I asked.

Ethan nodded, dabbing my swollen lips with antiseptic wipes.

"Do you need my Health Card number?"

Ethan smirked, opening the tube of Polysporin.

"You have good bedside manner, Dr. Stinson," I said.

Ethan put down the tube. "You ain't seen nothing yet," he said and kissed my neck.

The phone rang. Ethan groaned and passed me the frozen corn, gesturing for me to hold it against my mouth while he answered the call.

"Hey, Dad," Ethan said into the phone. His face fell. "Are you serious? They're going to keep her overnight? ----You're *both* staying?----No, don't come home just for me----I'm okay. Christmas can wait----I'm glad everything's going to be okay. Give Ellie a hug for me----Bye."

I took the corn off my face. "Something wrong?" I asked.

Ethan sighed. He rejoined me on the couch and pulled the blanket up over the two of us. "Sometime between the X-ray and the cast, Ellie spiked a fever. She's probably just tired; that happens sometimes. They started her on Tylenol and I.V. antibiotics. She perked up right away, but they want to keep her overnight for observation. My parents are going to stay in town." Ethan wrapped his arms around me and drew me to him. "Can I come to B.C. with you?" he whispered in my hair.

I knew he wasn't serious, that he'd never leave Ellie, not while she was so sick. Ellie was Ethan's number one woman and that was okay by me. "It's tough for you, too, isn't it?" I asked, though it wasn't really a question.

Ethan sighed again. "How can you love someone so

much, worry about them constantly, but be jealous of them at the same time? I'll be eighteen in three months; aren't I a little old to still be fighting for my parents' attention? Times like this, I wonder how things might be different if my first mom and dad hadn't died, if Ellie wasn't my sister but just the sick kid next door. I wonder if one day something I experience or accomplish could be at least as important as her CF. Do I want to find the cure to save Ellie and other kids like her, or just to impress my parents?" Ethan's voice broke. "God, I'm so selfish. My sister is in the hospital and I'm sulking like a preschooler because I got left alone on Christmas Eve."

"Ethan," I said. "You're not alone."

# Chapter 18

Ethan woke me Christmas morning just as the sun was poking its nose above the eastern horizon. He was already up and dressed and had fetched my clothes—they'd been washed and dried and no longer told tales of last night's cold, wet anti-adventure.

"Ho Ho Ho," he said and mussed my bed head.

"Hey! Merry Christmas." I stretched and yawned, then grimaced as pain shot through my jaw, reminding me of things I'd rather forget.

"Your mother's here," Ethan said.

*"Here?"*

"In the kitchen. I saw headlights come up the driveway about an hour ago. You were snoring so loud I couldn't sleep," Ethan chuckled.

"I do *not* snore," I said, then grasped the peril of the situation. "My *mother* is *here*, in your kitchen?"

Ethan nodded. "I made coffee, tried to calm her down a little. I had to keep her from storming the house to see where I'd harboured you."

"Is she furious?"

"She was out-of-her-mind worried when she first got here, wanting to know if I'd heard from you. She's pretty pissed off now that she knows you're fine. You should have told her where you were, Tee, or at least let her know you were okay," Ethan said.

I sighed. "I tried her cell phone last night like she asked, but there was no answer. They make you turn them off in the hospital." It was a stupid reply and Ethan knew it. I could have left a message at the desk or on our answering machine at home.

"You should probably get dressed and go talk to her."

I put my head back in the pillow and groaned. It had been so nice just to forget about everything for a while. "Thanks for the warning, Ethan," I said. It was one thing for my mother to know I'd spent the night at Ethan's, something else altogether if she barged into his room now and found me lazing in bed dressed in his Joe Boxers and an old undershirt.

Ethan kissed the top of my head. "I'm going to take Bert for a run in the field, give you two some time alone. My dad called—they won't be home until after eleven, so take your time. Good luck."

When he left, I hurriedly dressed and snuck a peek in the mirror. My bottom lip was swollen and crusted with dried blood, my left cheek was puffed out the way it had when I got my wisdom teeth out. The fact Ethan could even look at me without gagging was a testament to how he felt about me, I guess.

"Merry Christmas," I said to Lucy and plunked down in a chair across from her at the kitchen table. Merry or not, it was definitely a Christmas to remember.

"Right," she said back, her face lined with worry and fatigue. Her expression softened when she looked up from her coffee mug and saw my pulverized face. "Oh, Jesus," she whispered.

"How's Dad?" I asked dully.

Lucy took another sip of coffee before responding. "Mel's okay—the medication has been discontinued. They're keeping him in the hospital a few days, trying another drug, seeing if they can achieve the desired results without the emotional side effects. But I don't want to talk about Mel right now, Theresa. I want to talk about you."

Here we go, I thought. Another birth control lecture. I'd save her the trouble. "Don't worry, Lucy, we used a condom." I had no idea why I said that. Ethan and I had shared his bed, but we hadn't *slept* together. What we had done was talk for hours; or rather, Ethan had talked. He told me stories about Newfoundland and the now-extinct Beothuk peoples, about fishing with his birth mother's father, Grandpa Joe, and about getting lost on a class trip to Signal Hill when he was eleven. He pointed out all the constellations in the glow-in-the-dark universe he'd constructed on his ceiling. Being careful of my face, he'd held me until I fell into an exhausted sleep.

Lucy sighed. "We can talk about that later; your sex life is not my main concern right now. My concern is that I got home this morning at four a.m. and you were gone, the canoe was gone, the Jeep was gone. There was no note indicating where you were. There was no message on the answering machine. Your dog was whimpering by the back door waiting to be let out. I was *terrified*, Theresa. I knew you were more upset than you let on about what happened, but I didn't think you'd do something crazy like run off without leaving a message for me."

"When I left the house I didn't intend to stay out all night," I explained. "I didn't even mean to come to Ethan's.

I was just going to ditch the canoe somewhere like you asked, then come home."

Lucy wasn't listening. "I tried your cell phone, but it rang and rang, and I know you never go anywhere without it. I even called the county hospital in case you'd changed your mind and decided to get your face checked out. I shouldn't have left you alone, Theresa. I'm so sorry." Lucy started to cry. It was weird how she could go from irate to repentant in five seconds flat; she would've made a good actress.

"Mel needed you with him. He was in no condition to tell the doctors what was wrong," I said truthfully.

"I never should have left you alone," Lucy repeated.

"How did you find me?" I asked in an attempt to move the discussion along. I didn't envy Lucy her job as my mother and Mel's ex-, soon-to-be second wife. No wonder she felt she needed a therapist.

Lucy reached into her purse for a tissue and blew her nose. "I just had a hunch you'd driven out to Georgina's property. She was always the strength of this family and I know how important she was to you, how much you miss her and that big goofy dog of hers. When I found the Jeep there, and your knapsack and cell phone, I panicked. I could see by the light of my headlamps the fresh tracks in the dirt and snow where you'd dragged the canoe down to the water. Theresa, what were you thinking? It's *December*. It's minus five out there, not counting the wind chill."

"I don't know," I said. "It was stupid, but I wanted to take the canoe out just once; I hated to see all that effort wasted. But the wind picked up. I got caught in the current and lost my paddle. I knew if I didn't panic, the river would guide me past Ethan's. I waited until I saw his house and bailed out."

"*You jumped in the river!* Theresa, you could have *drowned!*" Lucy yelled.

"I know."

"You weren't *trying* to kill yourself, were you?" Lucy looked horrified.

I shrugged. "I knew the rapids were up ahead. I figured it was better to bail and take my chances at swimming to shore. And I wanted to talk to Ethan."

Lucy nodded. "I know you trust him. I hoped you'd contacted him, let him know where you were going. That's why I came here. If Ethan didn't know, I was going to call the police."

"I'm sorry I worried you," I said.

Lucy wasn't looking for an apology. "Why didn't you call me, Theresa? Let me know where you were? That you were okay?"

"Dr. Spellman would say it was because I wanted to punish you."

"Is that true?"

I took a deep breath, then let it out. "No. I just wanted to get away for a while. To think things through. To be with Ethan."

Lucy was quiet for a long while. "Ethan's pretty special, isn't he?"

I nodded. "Yeah. I'm going to miss him so much I get a stomach ache just thinking about it."

"Is he going somewhere?" Lucy raised a brow.

"No, I am."

Both brows went up. At this rate, Lucy was in for some serious forehead wrinkles. "What?" Clearly she wasn't up for any more surprises, but she had to know.

"I'm going to accept the early-admittance offer from B.C. and start my under-grad studies right away. It's what's best, I think, for all of us."

Lucy sucked in her breath. "When do you leave?"

"New Year's Day. Orientation begins the sixth of January. If Mel won't let me take the Jeep, I've got enough from what Aunt George left me to get a car and still cover my tuition and residence fees."

Lucy shook her head. "You know Mel wants to pay for your education."

"Whatever." I wasn't in the mood to haggle over money. His or mine. It was mostly Aunt George's anyway. I was just glad Lucy wasn't making an issue of me driving out West on my own.

"Theresa, New Year's is only a week away."

"Yeah." I shrugged.

Lucy took a sip of coffee and started to cry again. A few minutes later, she wiped her eyes, smiled at me, and took a deep breath. "I understand why you need to do this."

"You do?" I asked. "Because it isn't to get away from Mel. I know he didn't mean to hurt me."

"No, but I understand what it's like to give up your own wants and dreams to try to make someone else happy," Lucy said. "And I know what it's like when it backfires. Theresa, it's time you stop worrying so much about Mel and concentrate on your own goals and your own plans. You've been dealt more grief in the past six months than some people get in a lifetime. And it can drain you of your spirit, until you're so full of guilt and resentment that you start doing stupid, rebellious things…like taking that damn canoe out on the river last night."

Lucy really did understand. "Is that why you cheated with Creepy Harold?" I asked.

"I don't know." Lucy sighed. "Probably. I can tell you I never loved 'Creepy Harold,' as you like to call him. But he paid attention to me, made me feel wanted and important during a time when your father was too busy with his work and with you to pay me any notice. I was angry with your father, but more angry at myself. I foolishly gave up so much when I got pregnant and married young. I quit university and lost contact with my friends in Montreal. I gave up an offer to work as a coach apprentice with Disney on Ice. And I was happy to do it. I wanted a baby and I loved Mel so much. It might have been okay if—"

I interrupted. "If I hadn't been such a brat."

"No, Theresa, if I'd been stronger, more assertive, less willing to give up everything for the promise of love. Lots of people, very happy people, can find ways to balance school and work and relationships and children. Your father and I both had problems with balance from the get-go. You know that's part of what we were working on with Dr. Spellman. We'll continue with a new therapist in Ottawa."

So Mel's "episode" last night wasn't going to send Lucy packing back to Toronto after all. "Were you glad to get divorced?" I asked.

Lucy chewed on her lip, taking a long time to reply. "No," she said. "Not at the time, in any case. I never stopped loving your father. But I think, in hindsight, I needed the time away to sort myself out. It wasn't until I left for Toronto that I realized how far my life had drifted from where I'd hoped it to be. There I was already in my thirties, with nothing to show for it but a job beneath my skills, a broken marriage, and a surly teenager who clearly and perhaps rightfully hated my guts."

"I'm sorry."

Lucy shook her head. "No, Theresa. None of this was ever your fault. My point is that when your path gets muddled, and I know that so many of your plans got derailed this year, not just the canoe trip, it helps to find a place for yourself away from the chaos. Going to Toronto did that for me—B.C. might do that for you. The time away made me see things more clearly, from a different perspective. I explored my needs, found and followed my own path, and for better or worse—mostly better despite how it feels right now—it led back to you and Mel. I'll miss you like crazy, but I'm so proud you have the strength to do now what I waited so long—too long—to do. You have my blessing, honey. Go chase your dream."

"Thanks." I touched her hand, then got up and poured myself some coffee. Out the kitchen window, I watched Ethan toss a Frisbee to Bert in the snow-covered field. For a fleeting moment I felt like the star of a Maxwell House commercial.

"What does Ethan think of your plans?" Lucy asked when I returned to the table.

I sighed. "He's upset, but I think he understands. He has big goals and plans, too. What do you think Mel will say?"

Lucy smiled. "Mel thinks you hung the moon, Theresa. He always has. It drives him nuts that the past few months have been so hard on you. He wonders sometimes if it might have been easier for you to cope if he'd flat-out died."

*"What?"* Tears sprung to my eyes.

Lucy took my hand across the table, but I snatched it back.

She sighed. "Sorry, Theresa, I shouldn't have said anything. Mel just meant that if he'd died, once you got over the anger and hurt, you would've been able to focus on the good memories of your past with him, like you can with your Aunt George. But Mel can't dwell on the past now—he needs us to help him deal with the future. He needs to move forward with his life and one of the best ways you can help him right now is to show him you are moving forward with yours. Bottom line, Mel will worry about you being so far away from home, but he won't try to stop you if it means you'll be happy...and getting a head start on your university education." Lucy paused and picked at her nail polish. Then she looked me in the eye. "Mel's very, *very* upset about hitting you. He wants you to call him this morning."

"He can call me."

Lucy sighed. "He's embarrassed, Theresa; he's always taken such pride in his self-control. If he saw your swollen face right now, he'd never forgive himself."

Oh, well, poor Mel, I thought. I got up and glanced out the window again at Ethan. There was a guy who understood balance. Who somehow made time for school, his family, work, and me. I thought about Thanksgiving morning when he'd shown up hungover at Aunt George's door. How he'd apologized for his sleazy come-on and was willing to do whatever he could to ease the tension between us. If he'd sat back that morning, expecting me to call him, he'd still be waiting today.

Ethan wasn't perfect, but he was becoming a good man, I was sure of it. By contrast, my father, it seemed, still had a lot of growing up to do. Sure, I'd call Mel often, I'd fly home for his wedding, I'd visit on holidays and each summer. I'd love him and wish him and Lucy only the best. I'd be there in times of crisis—though I hoped there'd be no more for a while. But I was no longer Daddy's Little Girl. I was free to be me, whoever that was. At last.

# Chapter 19

Mel was discharged from the hospital December 30th, the afternoon before New Year's Eve. I'd called him a few times to say hello and to tell him about my B.C. decision, but I hadn't seen him. I hadn't really left the house at all since that night on the river, except to visit Ethan when I knew his parents wouldn't be home. Nothing short of a bag over my head those first few days could have disguised the fact that someone had punched me in the mouth, and it only looked worse as the bruises turned from purple to blue to green to yellow. I didn't want the Stinson parents worrying that Ethan was dating a tough chick, or worse, a sad girl from a violent home.

I couldn't avoid Ellie; with the funky purple cast on her left wrist, she was home with Ethan most of the week while the schools were on break and her parents were at work. I briefly considered telling her I'd whacked myself with a door or had a minor car accident, but in the end I felt she was mature enough to hear the truth. The morning of Mel's discharge I stopped by Ethan's for a while; I was too anxious to wait for Mel at home. Ellie asked if I'd ever forgive my father for hitting me.

"It wasn't really his fault," I said. "He was upset about the canoe and couldn't control his anger. It was bad drugs that made him hit me."

Ellie's eyes grew wide. "Like cocaine?"

I laughed. "No, just some medication for his muscles that he got at the hospital. He was allergic to it or something."

Ellie nodded solemnly. Medical glitches were hardly news to her. Then she brightened. "I still think you're pretty," she said.

I laughed. "You need glasses."

Ellie grinned. "Nope. My eyesight is perfect—not like old Monkey Ears over there." She gestured to Ethan who was dredging the kitchen cupboard for munchies.

Ethan and I hadn't talked much in recent days about my leaving for B.C., but as my departure time grew near, I knew it weighed on our minds. Ethan was quieter and less comical than usual, but he always seemed glad to see me when I stopped by. He sometimes talked about his own plans for a busy spring as if to reassure me, or maybe himself, that he wouldn't be moping around counting the hours until my return to North Creek. Ethan needed only two more credits to graduate. He was taking French and Calculus in the mornings and working his farm job in the afternoons Monday to Friday and all day Saturday to save for university. For extra school credit, he'd also arranged a twice-weekly evening co-op placement at the North Creek After-Hours Clinic. Ethan figured he'd be watering plants, making coffee, arranging magazines, and taking out the trash. But he had a keen eye and knew how to ask questions; he hoped that sooner or later someone would let him into the basement labs and show him how the machines worked.

"Ethan's going to build a Frankenstein Monster one day." Ellie was clearly in awe of her brother's interest in genetics. There was no doubt in my mind that Ethan could do anything he set his mind to.

"Maybe he could make you a Justin Timberlake Monster," I grinned.

"Do you think?" She looked over at Ethan, raising a hopeful brow.

"Right after I make a Tee Monster for myself," Ethan laughed, but there was sadness in his eyes.

I drove home just before noon. Lucy was back from Ottawa and had Mel settled in the house when I arrived. There was Chinese take-out, my favourite, laid out on the kitchen table.

I'd checked my face in the mirror of the sun visor before leaving the Jeep. My mouth didn't look too bad by then. The swelling was gone and the yellowed bruising was faded enough so it could be obliterated with generous globs of concealer. I hated wearing so much makeup—I felt like a clown—but damn if I'd let Mel see the leftovers of what he'd done to me in his anger. I didn't know whether I was protecting Mel from guilt or protecting my own dignity.

During lunch, Lucy guided the discussion. She stuck to what she considered upbeat topics, like my decision to go to B.C. Both she and Mel agreed it would be a great head start on my post-secondary education, an adventure, and an opportunity to exercise my growing independence. Mel played along with Lucy's enthusiasm, but he could sense there was something different about me now, something he found unsettling. He knew I no longer shared his mind; I had my own.

At the same time, I sensed that my departure would bring him some relief. I'd given it a lot of thought and acknowledged, at least to myself, that I'd put too much pressure on Mel when I went ahead with the canoe project despite his wishes. He needed more rest now, more time to do basic things like taking a shower, turning the pages of a book, or typing on his new computer. Mel didn't need reminders of the past. He needed help and encouragement through his recovery, and Lucy, to her credit, knew how much, how often, and how to in a way that preserved Mel's dignity and sense of humour. He'd been through so much these past few months and rather than adapt with him, I'd spent much of my time clinging to the past, moaning about how his physical limitations and amnesia affected and inconvenienced *me*. I came up short in the empathy department time and again.

After lunch, Mel took me aside and apologized "for what happened." I guess he couldn't bring himself to say "for bashing you in the mouth with my fist." I'd planned to say something long-winded and philosophical, but in the end I just told him it was okay, not to worry about it.

"Can we forget it happened?" Mel asked.

What was it with the guys in my life thinking selective amnesia was an appropriate conflict management strategy? Mel of all people should have known better. "No," I sighed, then leaned over and kissed his cheek. "But we can go on from here. I still love you, Dad."

Mel, Lucy and I spent the afternoon opening the Christmas gifts that had been abandoned under our tree in the wake of Mel's tirade and subsequent hospitalization. My gifts were the usual fare: clothes from Lucy, books from Mel. I'd bought Lucy a pair of funky silver earrings and a silk scarf weeks ago in Toronto, and in lieu of the canoe, I'd hurriedly ordered Mel an Eddie Bauer sweater on-line, which had been delivered to the house the previous afternoon.

The rest of the day was spent sorting my finances and going over the details of my travel plans, course selections, and accommodations in B.C. Mel agreed to sign the Jeep over to me, saying he'd rather have me driving across the country in an old but reliable vehicle than trusting something new. I'd be studying five subjects, all sciences—it would be a grind, but would keep me focused. With the over-the-phone help of the university housing office, I'd leased a small off-campus apartment that allowed pets. Ernie was growing into a huge hulk of a retriever, already a muscular sixty-five pounds at just six months old. Mel and Lucy were glad he was going with me; they considered him added security against God-knew-what might lurk out on the West Coast and prey on underage coeds. I wasn't afraid; at that point, I figured I'd seen it all.

New Year's Eve morning passed in a blur. I finished my last-minute packing and lugged my boxes and bags out to the Jeep while Lucy drove Mel into the Centre for an out-patient appointment. I'd packed light; my apartment was furnished and Mel had given me a supplemental card so I could charge whatever else I wanted to his Visa. Thank you, Aunt George, I said to myself. It was true that money couldn't buy happiness, but it could get me a nice futon and some matching towels for my bathroom.

Ethan picked me up at noon and took me to the city for New Year's lunch, all-you-can-eat Italian at Crazy Louie's. Neither of us referred to it as our official "Goodbye Lunch," but there was no mistaking the heavy undercurrent as we dug into plates of lasagna, veal scaloppini, Caesar salad, and garlic bread.

After our meal we took a long walk by the semi-frozen canal—the world's longest skating rink wouldn't be open for business for another week or two—and talked. When we reached the Dow's Lake Pavilion, we held each other and cried until we laughed.

"Is it going to be this hard leaving each other every time we're together?" I asked, kissing him on the mouth to let him know my face was better; my lips were back in business.

"I hope so."

"You know what we're going to do after my parents' wedding?" I asked.

Ethan raised a brow.

I pointed back towards the canal. "I'm going to teach you to skate."

Ethan and I arrived back in North Creek a little after six and stopped by the video store. Some kids from school were there, so we chatted awhile about Toronto and my plans to head directly to university. I wasn't the only North Creek senior to have completed my credits; I wasn't even the only one heading West. Len Goning had plans to work at his uncle's computer company in Calgary until he saved enough money for business college. None of the kids stared at my face or seemed uncomfortable talking to me; fortunately, everyone in town had been too busy with their own holiday agendas to have paid much attention to the loud goings-on at the Stanfords.

From the video store, we picked up Ellie, who was visiting a school friend in town, and headed back to my place. Thankfully, my parents were going out; Mr. Harnett was back from his trip and had invited Mel and Lucy over for a low-key New Year's party. Lucy had tipped Mr. Harnett off about the canoe episode. He'd been concerned, particularly about me, but in the end, he promised not to bring it up with Mel.

Lucy called me into her bedroom where she was doing her hair. Ethan was making popcorn and talking to Mel in the kitchen about the credibility of the latest cloning reports in the newspapers. Ellie was in the den deciding which movie to put on first. We'd be sticking to comedies. We had only look to our own lives for drama and horror. "We'll be back very late," Lucy said.

"Okay," I shrugged.

Lucy set down her hairbrush and turned to me. "I was a little surprised Ethan brought his sister over. Don't the two of you want to be…alone…what with it being your last night and all?"

"We were alone all afternoon," I said.

"I know, but…never mind. I should just mind my own business." Lucy stood up, smoothed out her slinky blue dress, leaned over and kissed my cheek. "Do you want me and Mel to stay home tonight? I'm sure Ron would understand."

I shook my head. "No, Lucy. You and Mel go out, have a good time. Mel needs to mingle. And I'm fine. Ethan and I are fine. Everything's fine." I tried to sound reassuring.

Lucy nodded and said, "I guess it's easier having Ellie here. I can understand how you might not want a long, drawn-out goodbye scene with Ethan, a tear-jerker filled with promises neither of you have the experience or resources to keep."

"Lucy, you watch too many old movies."

It was a special occasion, so Ellie had been given permission to forgo her tube feeding for the night.

"But Mom says I have to make sure to eat *lots* of greasy junk food," she said, looking hesitant.

I passed her a plate of homemade nachos dripping with cheese and sour cream. "Tough life, kid."

Ellie grinned, swallowed a fist full of enzyme capsules, and dug right in.

We watched two videos, laughing and eating till we thought we'd burst. Then, bundled against the wind, we took Ernie for a romp in the yard. We trooped back in when we got cold, made hot chocolate, and watched another video until Ellie fell asleep on the floor, snuggled next to the dog, just a little after eleven.

"I should get her home," Ethan said, making a move to rise from the couch where he and I were stretched out. "Come on, Ellie." He nudged her gently with his big toe.

Ellie sat up. "I'm awake," she yawned, glancing up at me and Ethan with bleary eyes. "We don't need to go just yet."

"Want to rest on my bed for awhile?" I asked her. "It's only a little while to midnight."

Ellie nodded, so I led her and Ernie down the hall to my room.

"Just so you know, I won't pee on your bed," Ellie assured me. "It's only sometimes, and *only* when I do my tube feedings."

"It's okay, kid. Even if you did, it wouldn't be the end of the world." I told Ellie a secret: Mel sometimes wet the bed, too, and that more than once while we were in Toronto, I'd heard Mel in the shower and Lucy in the laundry room in the wee hours. I'd never said anything about it; Mel would be embarrassed if he knew I knew.

Ellie plunked down on my bed. Ernie jumped up and

settled beside her. She stared up at the ceiling, suddenly pensive.

"Everything okay?" I asked.

She smiled at me, brushing a strand of dark hair from her eyes. "Sure. I had fun tonight. Thanks for letting me come." A pause. "It's easier with me here, isn't it?" she asked.

"What is?" I asked, playing dumb.

"Saying goodbye to Ethan."

I shook my head. "I'll be back in six weeks, Ellie. At least for a weekend. You and Ethan are invited to my parents' wedding."

Ellie shrugged. "I know."

I pushed Ernie over a little and lay down on the bed, too. "Then what's wrong, kiddo? Spill it."

Ellie shrugged. "Ethan's really upset, more than he's letting on. *Way* more than he was when he had to leave Tina. I think he's *madly* in love with you," she whispered.

"You think?" I asked, not entirely displeased.

Ellie nodded. "Christmas night, on my way to the bathroom for the ten millionth time, I heard choking noises coming from Ethan's room. I thought maybe he was sick, so I snuck in to see him. It's weird; whenever Ethan gets sick with the flu or whatever, he never gets any attention for it from Mom and Dad. He doesn't have a fatal disease, so they figure it's no big deal. But sick is sick, right?"

"*Was* he sick?" I asked, already aware that Ethan's needs often came up short on his parent's list of priorities.

Ellie shook her head. "He was…crying. I hadn't seen Ethan cry like that since he was eleven and his Grandpa Joe died. They were real close, used to go fishing and go-carting and stuff. Ethan's afraid of losing you, Tee."

I sighed. "Did he tell you that?"

"No…he told me to 'get the hell out of his room' and

leave him alone...but...I feel bad anyway."

"Because?"

Tears suddenly filled Ellie's eyes. "Because he's going to lose me—hopefully not for a while—but it's 'inevitable' is what the doctor's say. It's not fair: Ethan lost his own parents, he's going to lose me, his last girlfriend was a cheating *airhead* who dumped him, and now you're leaving him, too!"

I rubbed her back, tried to dispel her fear. "Ellie, I'm not leaving Ethan. Like I told him, I'm leaving town to go to school, and to sort out some of my family problems. Ethan will like me better when I'm not so sad and angry and crying all the time. He won't see me every day, but when we do see each other we'll be able to do fun stuff, joke around, plan our futures together. Sure, we'll miss each other, but..."

"I'm going to miss you, too, Tee," Ellie sniffed.

"Kid, you couldn't get rid of me if you tried; we're related."

"How's that?" Ellie asked.

I grinned and ruffled Ernie's ears. "Your dog and my dog are brothers."

Ethan burst into the room then. By his face, I could tell he'd overheard most of my conversation with Ellie. But he played it cool.

"Hey, my two favourite chicks!" he exclaimed. Nudging Ernie onto the floor, Ethan wedged himself between Ellie and me, putting a strong arm around each of us. Five minutes later, we were all fast asleep. We slept through the midnight bells at the church, through Lucy and Mel coming home, through Lucy pulling my comforter over the three of us and phoning the Stinson's to tell them Ethan and Ellie were spending the night. I didn't open my eyes until the next morning when Lucy shook me awake and told me it was seven a.m., time to go.

# Chapter 20

New Year's morning dawned bright and bitterly cold with a razor sharp wind from the north. If I hadn't had ten hours of driving ahead of me—my first scheduled stop was at Sault Ste. Marie—it might have been tempting to lie in bed all day with a mug of frothy hot chocolate and a good book.

The goodbye scene was blessedly short. Ellie was wheezy and needed to get home for her morning mask treatment and postural drainage, her "thumps" as she called them.

I hugged her, gave her my e-mail address, and told her we'd get together the morning of the wedding, just the two of us, no boys allowed, to do each other's hair. It wasn't much, but I wanted to give her something tangible to hold onto. I knew her parents would never let her visit me on the West Coast, even if Ethan was along; her health was too fragile for cross-country tripping. I wasn't sure how we'd become so important to each other; it went beyond Ethan, a puppy, and some boy advice. Ellie was a kid who loved her life despite all the crap she'd experienced and would continue to experience. She didn't pretend to be happy all the time, didn't enjoy the extra attention she got for being sick, didn't like that her disease set her apart from her friends. But she still had a compassion for others, a sense of humour, and a spunky, creative soul. She had the wisdom to acknowledge she'd been dealt a bad hand but the spirit not to fold too soon. The lessons she taught me about courage and resilience would stick with me all my life.

Ethan gave me a quick kiss and whispered something in my ear. I nodded and gave him a conspiratorial wink. In a blink, he was pulling out of the driveway, Ellie waving wildly out the rear window. Lucy and Mel stood in the doorway, baffled that Ethan's quick departure hadn't turned me into a crying, clingy mess.

Lucy hugged me for a long time and I found myself not wanting to let go. We'd become closer since the episode with Mel and our long talk Christmas morning. We had a ways to go before anyone confused us with Joan and Melissa Rivers (thank God), but I liked to think we might one day be friends.

Lucy had confided she hadn't and wouldn't tell Mel about my temporary insanity the night I took the canoe down the river; it would only worry him. I'd also humoured her, letting her give me a birth control lecture. It wasn't her advice—which was, after all, just a rehashing of what I'd already known for *years*—that meant the world to me. It was the support she assured me I'd receive from her if I did one day find myself young and unexpectedly pregnant the way she had her first year of university. I told Lucy that Ethan and I weren't planning to close the deal any time soon. We had too much on our agendas in the next few months, maybe years, to worry about all the what-ifs and difficult decisions, to take on more than we already were. The look I received from Lucy was not one of relief, but of amused skepticism.

I brushed away Lucy's goodbye tears, assuring her I'd be

joining a gym to work off my academic stress; I was still anti-booze and knew this would cost me socially with the party-go-lucky frosh crowd. I mentioned I'd called Deena at the Centre and asked for a referral to a Vancouver youth group or counselling centre; I wanted to start sorting out some of my jumbled emotions before my parent's wedding. It had taken me awhile, but now I understood that asking for help could be a sign of strength.

"Be safe," Lucy said when I pulled away at last. "I love you."

I gave her a quick kiss on the cheek. For the first time I could remember, I replied, "I love you, too, Mom."

Mel's goodbye was brief and full of fatherly advice. Don't let the gas tank get below a quarter. Don't drive after dark. Check in every morning and night until arriving at the university. Keep tabs on the weather channel; don't be afraid to wait out a storm even if it means arriving in B.C. a few days late. Take it slow and steady over the mountains. He didn't tell me to watch out for the other guy; he was one of those guys now, and he knew it. "I love you, Theresa-Jean," Mel said. "I'm so proud of you." For the first time in my life, I saw tears in his eyes.

"I love you, too," I said, hugging him close. He was no longer Superman, but he was still my Dad.

As planned, Ethan met me at the lock station. He was outside, his nose pink with cold, leaning against Wilma's passenger door when I parked the Jeep and joined him. Ernie stayed in the back seat, barking his head off. He knew all the packing and hugs hadn't been for a fifteen-minute ride down the road and he was eager to keep moving.

"It's over here," Ethan said, taking my hand and leading me down a small slope to the lock house.

The canoe looked great; aside from a few long scrapes and rock gashes on the hull's underside, it was like new. It hadn't catapulted down the steep rapids after all. Something that night, some unknown force, had caused it to veer out of the main channel and into the canal. A Parks Canada employee had found it penned by ice against a lock during his rounds. He'd called the police immediately to see if any missing persons reports had been filed, but there were none, and it wasn't unusual for boats carelessly tied or stowed near the river to be swept downstream in foul weather. Realizing the canoe must have drifted from a private dock upstream, he'd spent the morning before the New Year scouting area farms to see if anyone knew who owned it.

Ethan had been outside tinkering with Wilma's carburetor when the man from Parks Canada pulled into the Stinson's driveway and asked if anyone had lost a cedar strip canoe. It was a beautiful piece of work, he'd said, adding that the boat still gleamed under a coat of new varnish despite having spent at least a few days out on the water exposed to the winter elements.

I helped Ethan secure the canoe to his truck bed, got in the Jeep, and led Ethan west past Smith's Falls to Port Elmsley.

The year-round superintendent at Merrywood Camp wasn't expecting anyone to pull up to his lodge that frigid New Year's morning, but he took one look at what we had to donate, pulled on gloves and a parka, and went to clear a spot in the boathouse, no questions asked. Fifteen minutes later, Mel's canoe looked positively majestic nestled amongst a dozen dented Grummans. It had found a home; one where it would be well cared-for and well-used by hundreds each summer. It had survived a year of uncertainty, devastation, and rejection, and now had an opportunity to prove itself. Ethan didn't say so, but I think he was secretly proud that his hard work hadn't gone to waste.

The superintendent thanked us profusely and invited us into his small lodge for breakfast, but we declined. I had a long drive ahead of me; I wanted to make it to Sault Ste. Marie before nightfall. Unable to send us off empty-handed, he ran to his kitchen and presented me and Ethan with fresh-from-the-oven cinnamon rolls wrapped in wax paper and two plastic travel mugs filled with hot apple cider.

Back up the road at the main gates, Ethan and I parked once again and got out of our vehicles. It really was goodbye now and I could feel a lump stinging the back of my throat.

"I have something for you," Ethan said. He pulled a small wooden box out of his pocket. The lid was intricately carved and hand-painted.

"Did you make this?" I asked, admiring the workmanship and fine detail.

Ethan grinned. "I made the box and did the carving. Ellie painted it. She wanted me to wait and give it to you when we were alone. Open it."

My heart was pounding so hard I swear I could hear its echo across the nearby cow fields.

But then I opened the box and laughed out loud; in it was a thin leather necklace. From it dangled an "Ethan Monster," no taller than two inches. Its body and glasses were formed of multi-coloured telephone wire, tiny clothes were sewn from felt remnants, and wavy blond hair had been trimmed from Bert. In the centre of the chest was an oversized candy heart. The whole thing had been dipped in polyurethane and left to harden.

"Ellie made this?" I asked. It was seriously adorable.

Ethan laughed. "No. I did. And it's not a voodoo doll; it's just my way of 'hanging around' across the time zones."

"I love it," I said, securing the pendant around my neck.

"It's okay if you want to wear it *under* your shirt," Ethan laughed.

Ethan and I held each other tight, until a lone transport truck driver passed on the highway and tooted his horn. "Happy New Year!" he shouted out the window.

We pulled apart, but something passed between Ethan and me then, something besides that persistent *ping, ping, ping*. It was the knowledge that what we had was good. It was the understanding that even if our individual lives played out like turbulent white-water adventures, when and if our rivers merged, things might be calm, cool, smooth sailing.

Ethan picked up our mugs from the hood of his truck, handed me mine. "Let's make a toast," he said.

I clinked my plastic mug to his. "To Mr. Toaste."

## THE END